Wrangling Her Cowboy

Silver Creek Ranch
Book 1

Peyton Banks

ISBN 978-1-956602-99-9

The Silver Creek Ranch

Forgotten military heroes who needed a helping hand re-entering the society they had been sworn to protect. The Silver Creek Ranch provided a space where these cowboys could work the land and get back in touch with the men they once were.

The battles of war left scars on each of them.

Healing was what these cowboys needed.

Who knew it would comprise the touch, kiss, and love of a good woman?

The Silver Creek Ranch is an interracial cowboy romance shared world. Each captivating story is filled with plenty of heat and will leave your heart racing with the desire to devour every one of them.

Wrangling Her Cowboy
Blurb

A broken cowboy...his shining light. Will she be enough to pull him out of the darkness?

Draven Harvey came home to Ironhaven, South Dakota, to settle down. The retired Marine was done with serving his country and just wanted a peaceful life working his father's ranch. The Silver Creek Ranch was for men like him—broken and needing help finding their place in society.

After his time in the military, he wants to be left alone. Ranching was to be his life.

Cashea Moss took notice of the grumpy town hero who came to the bar where she sang every weekend. She was new to town, but she'd heard plenty about Draven. His eyes were intense and held tales of horror she was sure he had experienced during deployments. There was something about him that made her want to see him smile.

Draven tried to fight the attraction he felt for Cashea, but she quickly dismantled the barriers he had constructed around himself. He couldn't get her out of his mind after one steamy night. Her soft touch made him want to do things he'd sworn he wouldn't do—become a protector and fall in love.

Wrangling Her Cowboy is a steamy interracial BWWM romance with a broken small town hero, a beautiful heroine and a HEA.

Chapter One

"I never knew what could have been worse: my son coming home from war in a pine box or my son coming home a shell of his former self," Andy Harvey said.

The older man looked every one of his sixty years. His hair was completely gray, and experience was embedded on his skin in the form of wrinkles. His father may be older, but he still handled the ranch with every hand who came to work for him.

Draven couldn't look at his father and he also didn't want to admit those words stirred something in him. He was afraid of what he would see if he did meet his father's eyes. Draven would never be considered a coward, but when it came to this moment, he just couldn't do it. So instead, he stared out at the acres of land that lay before them. Night-time was upon them, and the dark sky was marred by the tiny twinkle of stars. He inhaled and blew out a deep breath. There was no way that he could look at the person who had raised him, taught him everything he knew about being a man, and see the disappointment in his eyes.

"I don't know what to say, Pops. I'm who I am," he replied dryly.

He leaned back against his pickup truck and folded his arms across his chest. Whatever fantasy his father had about who he would be after returning home from multiple deployments and war was just that—a fantasy. This was who Draven Harvey was, and he wasn't going to apologize either. He'd come home a year ago having retired from the Marines. He'd given his life to his country, and now it was time for him to live his in peace. The day he'd turned eighteen, Andy had escorted him down to the recruitment office so he could sign up to serve. Draven hadn't known what he wanted to do with his life so it had been suggested he enter the service. It was an honorable thing to do, and he could figure out later which direction he went in.

Twenty-four years he'd given.

Now he lived on the ranch his father had

purchased when Draven was seven years old. The Silver Creek Ranch had a sole purpose, and it was to help men and women like Draven who had come home from war broken. It was to give them a purpose in life. Help them acclimate back into society. Give them skills they could take and move on to do something else in life besides serve.

Draven had nothing but respect for his father and the ranch he had built. Draven had come home and hadn't hesitated to join in on working the ranch. The hard work allowed him to stay busy. The exhausting work even helped him escape the nightmares that plagued him once his head hit the pillows. The horrors of war still haunted him.

"You've been home for a year, son, and all you do is work. You do know I employ plenty of men and women to run this ranch. You don't have to do it all." Andy sidled up next to him. He reached out and rested a hand on Draven's shoulder.

Draven tensed for a moment. The hand disappeared from him. He glanced over at his father and saw nothing but sadness in his blue eyes that were the same as Draven's.

"I do more than work, Pops." Draven ran a hand along his face. He glanced at his watch and took in the time. If he hurried, he could get his seat at the bar he liked going to.

"Drinking your pain away doesn't count, Draven."

His father's voice was stern and reminded Draven of when he and his brother, Ridge, would get in trouble. Andy had been the disciplinary parent. Their mother, Flo, had been an angel and always felt her boys could do no wrong.

"You need to live life. Find a good woman to settle down with. Start a family. I imagine when I get older you would be taking over Silver Creek. If your mother were here she'd agree with me."

Thank God, she wasn't here to see him now. Martha "Flo" Harvey died a little over ten years ago from an aggressive form of cervical cancer. She would be torn up if she saw him. His mother had been a saint. She always had a smile on her face, a big heart, and always made the Harvey men feel as if they could do anything.

Draven struggled with his inner demons. The time in the service had taught him many things, but his father was right. It had changed him. He had joined Marines, and they had trained him to become a weapon for war. His training, the deployments, the battles, the kills...it did something to a man. Changed him. Caused him to lose his soul. Draven just hoped that once it was his time to leave this earth that there was a place in Heaven for him, but he seriously doubted it. The things he'd done for his country would probably earn him a nice cozy spot in Hell.

His father could never understand what he'd been through, what'd he'd done, all in the name of their beautiful country. There were some things he would never want his father to know. If Andy did ever find out, there would be more than sadness in those eyes.

"Believe me, there isn't enough alcohol to take it away, but dulling it does help." Draven pushed off the truck and ran his hand through his still-damp hair. He was just going to go down to the Hen House, the popular bar in town that always had decent beer on tap and a pretty good burger. Their televisions were large, and they would have the game on. That's all Draven wanted to do to wind down after a hard week of working the ranch. It was the weekend, and they normally had a cover band playing on Friday nights. He could ignore them as long as the game was on.

"Why don't you watch the game here? Come up to the house. Bee has cooked—"

"I'm good, Pop. I'm going out to unwind and get away for a bit. I promise to be on my best behavior." Draven smirked. He walked over to the driver's door of his oversized pickup truck and opened it.

"That's what I'm worried about. Just shoot me a text when you get home," Andy muttered. The older man stepped back, away from the truck.

Draven grinned. It didn't matter that he was forty-two years old, his father still cared about his boys. Andy gave a nod to Draven before turning on his heel and heading toward his truck. Draven watched his father drive along the road that led to the main house. It was the house where he and his brother had been raised.

Draven got into his vehicle and slammed the door shut. He hated the disappointment that showed in his father's eyes. Maybe he should have taken the old man up on the offer to watch the game with him. It wouldn't have hurt to have a beer with Pops and watch the game. Maybe next time.

Draven needed to get away from the ranch. He pretty much didn't go anywhere else. Not that he really complained. Draven enjoyed being back in Ironhaven. It was the small town he'd grown up in and where he felt most comfortable. In the Marines, he'd been based in many cities and towns around the world, but nothing compared to his roots. The place where he had been born.

He started the truck and threw it in gear. He drove along the road on the ranch that led to the main road. His father had wanted his boys to both stay near him. On the ranch, both Draven and Ridge had homes built on the stead. This was their legacy, and it felt damn good to know his father would trust him to continue on his dream.

Draven rolled down the window and enjoyed the wind on his face. The radio was on a country station that was currently playing an old Willie Nelson song. He felt himself relax as the music drifted along the air. His thoughts turned to the cover band that played at the Hen House. They were pretty good. He tried to not pay them too much attention when he was there, but their lead singer was beautiful and had a voice that captured everyone's attention. He didn't know her name and didn't recognize her. She must not have grown up here. Her smooth light-brown skin seemed to glow, her lips were curled up into a wide grin. She always appeared happy, and the crowd flocked to her when she got off the stage.

Draven shook his head. He attempted to push all thoughts of the siren from his head. A woman was not what he needed now, no matter what his father thought. He grimaced and tried to think of the last time he'd even been with a female. He wasn't any good for a woman. He was fucked up in the head. Hell, he barely knew how to be in society, much less know how to court a woman.

Draven concluded that he was just going down to the Hen House for exactly what he'd told his father. To get away from the ranch, have a drink with the locals, and watch the game.

That was all.

The drive to town wasn't long. Draven pulled his pickup truck into a parking spot at the back of the lot. His truck had been purchased brand-new, and he'd be damned if some fucking drunk knocked it because they couldn't hold their liquor. He killed the engine and stepped out of his vehicle. There were already a ton of cars parked in the lot which led him to believe that he was right in arriving at this time.

He slid his keys in his jeans pocket and headed toward the bar. A few people lingered outside the building. He ignored them and swung open the door. The aroma of good food and cigarettes greeted him. The bouncer, Ted, stood near the door. He tipped his chin to Draven who returned the move. Draven continued on toward the bar. He bit back a grimace at how many people were already in the place.

He quickly scanned the establishment, having already memorized every exit. He took in a few men who looked as if they would be giving Ted and his crew trouble tonight. Old habits died hard. It had been Draven's job for years to notice the littlest of details. That had saved his and his battalion's life more than once.

His gaze drifted toward the stage where the band was setting up. He didn't see the lead singer around. He tore his eyes away and focused on his destination. He arrived at the bar and glared at a few young punks standing near his favorite seat. They appeared to be college brats who barely had enough fuzz on their faces. They fell into a fit of laughter, and Draven grew even more irritated.

"Move," he growled.

The two facing Draven froze in place. Their eyes widened as they took him in. The one nearest him whose back was to him spun around.

"Who the fuck—" His words died as he found himself looking at Draven's chest. He paused and slowly tilted his head back to meet Draven's eyes.

He took a step back and jerked his head in a nod. "Yes, sir. Didn't mean to be in your way, sir."

The three of them immediately hightailed it away from the bar and disappeared in the crowd. Draven shook his head and plopped down in his chair. The other patrons around the bar were regulars. He nodded to them. He glanced up, and it warmed his heart to find the television already on the football game.

"I was wondering if you were going to show up." Danny chuckled. The older bartender slid an empty glass across the counter. He already had Draven's favorite bourbon in his hand. He poured a hefty amount and tipped his head to Draven.

Draven had known Danny almost his whole life. The bartender had gone to high school with Andy. His gray hair was kept cut close to his head, and the thick mustache was a legend.

"Appreciate this," Draven murmured. He lifted the glass and took his first sip. Now this was what he needed after a long day on the ranch. There was nothing like a good bourbon, and Danny always ensured he stocked the best.

"Well, I'm glad you came on over. Those kids get on my damn nerves, wanting the latest drinks they saw on social media. Who the hell do they think I am?" Danny snorted.

Draven rolled his eyes. He didn't know how Danny tolerated the younger crowd. His eyes gravitated toward the screen. As much as he liked conversing with Danny, he enjoyed watching football even more.

"You want your usual for supper?" Danny asked, pushing away from the counter.

"Yes, sir." Draven tilted his glass to Danny, unable to take his eyes off the television. The game was just getting started. He settled in and became engrossed. His concentration was broken by the small roar from the crowd behind him, then music filled the air. Whistles and clapping followed quickly. The partiers sounded as if they were ready to get down tonight.

"How are y'all doing tonight?" A husky voice floated through the speakers.

Draven stiffened as the siren's voice washed over him. He wanted to close his eyes and just soak up the sound of her voice. A few women screamed back their responses, then laughter followed. Draven refused to turn around. As much as he wanted to see her, he managed to sit still. Her angelic voice began singing an upbeat song. From the sounds of stomping and footsteps, people were already on the dance floor. People loved her and the band. Each Friday night the place was packed for their performance.

A figure sidled up next to Draven and waved Danny over. Draven set his empty glass down and looked at the newcomer invading his space. He hated when people got close to him. Didn't they know they shouldn't sneak up on a soldier—former soldier?

Draven was trained in the deadliest of combat and could seriously hurt someone. That was his gift from the Marines. The intense training he had undergone had left him a killing machine. He blinked a few times, trying hard to not fall down into memory lane. He unclenched his hand that had somehow balled into a fist.

Tom Cook, a sheep farmer who's land was on the other side of town, met his gaze. Draven relaxed slightly. The farmer was not a threat. He did a quick perusal of the area and found everyone at the bar focused on the televisions. Draven pushed down the urge to shake Tom's hand off him.

"Danny, put Draven's next drink on my tab," Tom said. He slapped Draven on the shoulder. The farmer's son had graduated a few years after

Draven. His son, Mark, had entered the Army and returned home after his first tour with one less leg.

"There's no need, Tom," Draven said.

Tom shook his head. "I don't want to hear it."

Danny came over and filled Draven's glass again.

"You sacrificed so much so that we can sleep in our beds at night safely," Tom said. "I'll buy you a damn drink if I want to."

"Many thanks." Draven's voice was gruff.

Tom patted him on the shoulder one last time before moving away. Draven hated the attention of the town. No one had to thank him for going to serve his country. It had been his decision. He lifted the glass and knocked it back. Fire burned his esophagus as the drink made its way down. He bit back a curse and turned around to get one glance at the stage. The siren's voice was calling to him. He'd get one quick look at her, then he'd turn around and get back to the game.

Chapter Two

Cashea Moss loved how people connected with her as she sang. She swung her hips around as she turned and faced Sara who was playing the hell out of her violin. It was Friday night, and the Hen House was crowded. The town always showed up when it was Friday. The dance floor was packed, and people were singing along with her.

Cashea liked to think it was to enjoy her and the girls. Their band, Haven's Chicks, was made up of a few locals who loved music as much as Cashea did. They were a cover band and damn good at it. They didn't write or perform any original music. This was a fun gig for all of them. Cashea and her bandmates had real jobs they worked during the week. They found time to get together to practice before performing on Friday and Saturday nights.

Cashea had had a love for singing for as long as she could remember. When she'd been a child, her father and grandfather would sit out in the yard around the fire pit singing old country songs. Her grandfather would play the banjo while her father loved his guitar. Those were fond memories she held near and dear to her heart. When her grandfather passed, she sang one of his favorite songs he'd taught her at his home going celebration.

She'd always had an ear for music. Cashea grew up singing in their local church, her schools choirs, and even in the glee team in high school. As much as she loved singing, too bad it didn't pay the bills. After relocating to Ironhaven, she'd gotten a job as a receptionist for a local pediatrician's office. She absolutely loved her job. It allowed her to connect with all of the families in town who had children, and her boss, Dr. Reddy, was an angel.

"Y'all know you know the words to this song. Help me out." Cashea laughed as the women down front, who must be well into their cups, hollered the words of a popular Reba McEntire song.

There wasn't much to do in Ironhaven, but they made the best of it. That was why Cashea had opted to settle here. She needed a change and she hadn't regretted it one bit. Ironhaven was a small town where pretty much everyone knew everyone. She had been accepted with open arms when she'd moved into her home. The welcome wagon of the neighborhood had rolled in full force during her first week. She had received so many casserole dishes, desserts, and bottles of alcohol that she couldn't even give them away. Her freezer was packed for months afterward.

Cashea had grown up in a town similar to Ironhaven, but she needed to make her own way away from her family. Even though she was thirty-five years old, her parents still tried to do everything for her. She loved them, she truly did, but she needed to spread her wings and fly. Their home had been one filled with love. Mom and Dad would be celebrating their forty-fifth anniversary next year. Cashea and her brother, Micah, had been the apples of their eyes. Micah, the eldest of the two, had been the best brother a girl could ask for. He'd entered the Marines after high school. She and her family couldn't be more prouder of him. She would send him so many care packages that he'd tell her to quit.

"*Are you trying to make me fat with all these snacks?*" his deep voice rumbled through the phone.

"*I'm just trying to make sure you get a piece of home while you are away.*" She laughed.

This deployment was to be for eighteen months. She missed him something fierce. She couldn't wait for the day for him to come home and stay. Permanently.

"*I appreciate it, but you're making the guys jealous. Do you know how many have asked if you're taken?*" He chuckled. "*I'm close to fighting every damn day to preserve your honor.*"

Cashea wasn't too surprised at that information. Her brother, who was three years older than her, had got into plenty of fights. He had a reputation of using his fists in school, but every single time was to protect those who couldn't protect themselves. That was just how honorable he was.

Six months later, her parents had gotten word that Micah had been killed in action. A part of Cashea had died the day she'd seen Micah in his casket. They were forever grateful to be able to have his body returned home so they could bury him next to her grandfather. Their town had even named a road in Micah's honor for his sacrifice.

That was another reason she'd had to leave home.

Shaking off the memories, she scanned the bar as the song came to an end. The next number was a little slower paced. Kim, their drummer, loved this song and had requested for Cashea to sing it. Cashea's gaze landed on a familiar figure sitting at the bar. His dark hair looked as if he'd combed his fingers through it several times. He sat in the same spot every Friday and Saturday night with his attention glued on the television while he ate and had a few drinks.

Draven Harvey.

She had heard plenty about the town hero. He'd grown up in this town, and they were so excited to have him back when he'd moved home. A year ago, around the time she'd relocated, they'd welcomed him home with a parade through the middle of downtown. He didn't look too happy then, but to think about it, she'd never seen him look happy. He always wore a scowl.

The dancers swayed to the music while she sang. Kim had chosen a great song for them to perform. Cashea added her own signature to each song. Her gaze went back to the bar, and she stood in shock.

He'd turned around.

She was too far away to see his eyes, but he was definitely facing her. He raised his glass and took a sip. She grew bold and tossed him a wink. Her heart thundered. Where did that come from? In the dark, smoky bar, she doubted he'd even seen it. He slowly swiveled back around, and once again, his back was to the stage.

Soon the song came to an end, and it was time for them to take their break. The crowd clapped, whistled, and cheered for them. Cashea grinned and took a bow. She placed the mic back in the stand and walked off the stage with her girls.

"Hey, I'm going to head to the bar," she said.

There was a little room where they stored all of their things and used as a hangout during their breaks. Kim waited for her while Sara, Lilly, and Monica headed to the back. The DJ of the bar took over and started playing an upbeat song to keep the patrons happy.

"Want me to come with you?' Kim asked.

"Nah. I'm going to grab a bottle of water. I won't be long," Cashea said.

Kim gave a nod and followed the other band

members. Cashea walked toward the bar. Butter-flies fluttered in her stomach. She didn't know why she was doing this, but something compelled her to go to the bar. She had a bottle of water in her bag in the back. She could have just drunk that, but instead, she found herself pulling into the empty space next to the grumpy cowboy.

"Hey, Danny." Cashea smiled while trying to wave the bartender down.

Danny spun round at the call of his name. He pushed away from the customer he had been chatting with and came down her way. She was thankful no one could see how nervous she was to be standing next to Draven. He was much taller and wider than she'd thought. This was the closest she'd ever been to him. From the stage he didn't appear to be this large. She certainly felt dainty beside him.

She felt his gaze on her, but she didn't acknowledge him. Her tongue snuck out and slid along her suddenly dry lips. Now she was here, she was having doubts. Did he like what he saw when he was looking at her?

Who was she kidding?

She was hot. She knew it. Everyone knew it. She bit back a snort.

"Hey, Cashea. What can I do you for?" Danny

asked. The older bartender was always so nice when she and the girls came to the bar. He'd worked here practically since the place had opened.

"Can I have a bottle of water, please?" she asked.

"Sure thing, doll." Danny walked away.

Unable to resist, she peeked over at Draven and found him staring at the television. She took the few seconds to study him. His strong jawline was covered with a light beard. His hair had a sprinkle of grays blended into the dark strands. Her fingers itched to run through his hair. She bit her lip taking in his solid build underneath his t-shirt and jeans.

Lord, she had a problem. Here she was, ogling a man who probably wouldn't even give her the time of day.

"You know it's impolite to stare," a deep, drawling baritone voice said.

Draven slowly met her gaze. Even in the low light of the Hen House, she was struck by his crystal-blue eyes. They were so clear they were almost iridescent. Her breath caught in her throat at the intensity in his eyes.

"Oh, um, I'm sorry," Cashea stuttered. He probably thought she had a few screws loose now. She blew out a deep breath and stretched out her hand. "Hi. I'm Cashea."

He stared at her hand for a long moment. She almost pulled back, thinking he wasn't going to shake it. Finally, his larger hand engulfed hers. His palms were callused, and her heart skipped a beat imagining his hands running along her skin.

"Draven." He removed his hand and turned back away from her and lifted his drink.

"I know who you are," she blurted out.

He glanced over at her with a raised eyebrow. She froze under his gaze that perused her body. Her nipples pushed against the material of her bra. She resisted the urge to shift her feet as he took her all in. She had chosen a summer dress with thin spaghetti straps and her worn-down pair of cowboy boots.

"Here you go, doll," Danny announced. He set the bottle on the counter.

Cashea reached for her water, thankful for the distraction.

"Thanks, Danny, and can you do me one more favor?" she asked, giving him her winning smile. She tilted her head to Draven. "Put his next drink on my tab."

"Sure thing—"

"You don't have to do that," Draven interjected. He raised his hand and shook his head.

Danny paused, his gaze bouncing between the two of them. She reached over and rested her smaller hand on his.

"I want to. My brother was a Marine, too, but he didn't make it home. So let me buy you a drink to welcome *you* home," she said softly.

Something passed through his eyes that she couldn't read. For a moment, she thought he was still going to resist. Instead, he jerked his head in a nod.

"Thank you," he murmured. He focused on her hand still resting on top of his.

She hadn't even realized how close she had gotten to him. She slipped her hand from his and gave him a warm smile. It wasn't often she brought up her brother to a stranger, but for some reason she'd felt the need to in that moment.

Danny slid a very generously filled glass to Draven and tipped his head to them before he walked away.

"I've heard about your father's ranch and I wish my brother would have been able to go to a place like that. He would have loved it," she said.

Her brother had loved nature and horses. He

would have enjoyed being able to work a ranch with other former military. Sadness filled her heart, but Micah had died doing something he'd believed in. He'd believed in the freedom this country offered and wanted to help protect that. He had always looked out for the little man, and him going off to war was not surprising to their family.

"I'm sorry for your loss," Draven said. He finished off the drink he'd been nursing.

"Thanks, but there is to be no moping around. Micah would have my hide if he knew I was sad about him dying." She chuckled. It had taken her a while to get to this point in life after her brother's passing. But it was the truth. He would be pissed to know she was sulking over him.

Draven's attention was back on the television screen. The other patrons around the bar hollered at one of the plays going down. Cashea wasn't much of a football fan. She knew a few things from growing up and it always being on while her father and brother watched it. But she had never been one to follow the teams. She couldn't tell you who any of the players were, much less which team they played on.

"Well, I guess I should be going. It was nice to

meet you," Cashea said. She just hoped he didn't think she was a weirdo. That's all she needed.

A figure slid in behind her a little too close. Cashea stiffened.

"Well, look who it is," a voice said.

She rolled her eyes. This was the last person she had hoped to run into. She faced the newcomer. Brett Falco was often at the Hen House. He was a drunk and always shouted lewd remarks at her while she was up on the stage. She had been happy when they had started their set tonight and she hadn't seen him.

"Why are you so close to me? Hasn't your momma taught you manners?" she snapped.

"She sure hasn't. Why don't you come and teach me something." He chuckled.

The smell of whiskey greeted her. Brett and his family owned the local hardware shop in the middle of town. He assumed he was God's gift to women and had been trying to get Cashea to go out with him for months now. Women did swoon over him with his short blond hair, brown eyes, and tall physique. Unfortunately for Brett, he just didn't do anything for Cashea.

"Boy, bye." She grimaced and made to walk away. It was almost time for her to sing. She'd meet the girls in the back for a moment before they had to go on stage.

"Hey, don't leave yet." Brett grabbed her by her arm and turned her to face him.

"Get your hands off me." Cashea tried to pull free from him, but he held on tight.

"You don't have to rush off so fast." He smirked.

He tried to bring her closer to him, but she resisted. His lips were curled up in a crooked grin which she was sure most women would fall for, but not her.

"I have to go, Brett. Release my arm." Her free hand gripped her water bottle tight. She wasn't afraid to use it as a weapon. She'd taken self-defense classes in the past. She'd had issues with an old stalker boyfriend when she had moved to Minneapolis some years ago. That time of her life seemed like a lifetime ago. Her ex hadn't taken the breakup too well and had stalked her. She'd enrolled in the local self-defense classes. Thankfully, she had never had to use the skills she'd learned. He had finally got the point and dated a woman who lived in his apartment building. Eyeing Brett, she knew she may be rusty, but she could defend herself.

"When are you going to go out with me?" he asked, ignoring her request for him to let her go.

"When are you going to let me go?" she countered.

She tugged on her arm again, but his grip only tightened. His smile disappeared. This time he yanked on her, and she lost her balance. She fell into him with her water bottle falling somewhere on the floor. The smell of cigarette and booze was stronger. She reared back and tried to not inhale.

"So, what? You think you're too good to go out with me?" he snarled into her ear.

She pushed away from him, but he didn't let her go far. His chest was solid and his hold on her unwavering.

"Brett, get your hands off her," Danny said. He rested his hands on the counter and glared at Brett.

"Mind your business, old man," Brett snapped. He stared at Cashea with a devilish grin. "We are just having a conversation, aren't we?"

"Which has been over." Cashea was two seconds from kneeing him in the balls. She was going to count to two, and if he didn't release her, he'd been singing a new tune. "Now let me go."

"You must be hard of hearing," a deep drawl came from behind Cashea.

She glanced over her shoulder to see Draven holding his glass. He was staring down at it, but it was obvious he was speaking to Brett. A shiver went down her spine at the calmness that resonated in his voice. It didn't match the tension in his body.

"I don't think the lady wants your hands on her."

"Fuck off, Harvey." Brett scowled.

Draven knocked back the rest of his drink before setting the glass on the counter. He swiveled in the chair; those ice-blue eyes of his had a different glint in them now. She couldn't read what it was, but it sure made her heart skip a beat. His intense gaze landed on Brett.

She had a funny feeling it didn't mean anything good for Brett.

"What did you say?" Draven's voice dropped even lower.

Now they were drawing a small crowd. Everyone who had been standing around the bar was watching them.

"Maybe it's you who is hard of hearing." Brett finally released her.

Cashea took a step back away from him. Her wrist was throbbing from how tight his grip had been. She brought it up to her chest and massaged it with her free hand to help smooth it. Draven's eyes narrowed in on her actions. His jawline hardened. She immediately stopped what she was doing and moved toward him.

"It's okay. I'm fine," she said. She attempted a smile, but it didn't seem to calm him any. This situation was about to go south fast. She needed to put a stop to it now.

"You need to apologize." It wasn't a request from Draven but a statement.

"For what? Trying to take her stupid ass out?" Brett barked a laugh.

Cashea's eyes widened.

Stupid ass?

He was on his own with Draven. She stepped to the side to ensure she was out of his way. He slowly stood from his chair and closed the gap between him and Brett. Draven had at least three to four inches on him.

"You don't want to fuck around with me, boy," Draven said.

A commotion sounded behind her. Security was plowing through the crowd and headed their way. Danny must have alerted them to the situation. Their spectators were growing even larger. Cashea's face warmed in embarrassment.

"Who the fuck you calling a boy—" Brett's words died off followed by a bang.

Cashea jumped and turned back. Draven's hand wrapped around Brett's throat. He had Brett pushed up against the bar. Cashea flew forward just as Ted and his men arrived.

"It's okay. Let him go," she said, resting her hand on Draven's arm. She tried to pull him off Brett, but it was like trying to move a solid wall. The muscles beneath her hand were taut and firm.

He didn't take his eyes off Brett's beet-red face.

"Break it up," Ted shouted.

He and his men converged on Draven and Brett. Cashea got pushed back as the four large security guards yanked Draven off Brett. Cashea's heart was racing a mile a minute. She didn't know how this had gone to hell and back so damn fast.

"You're fucking crazy," Brett shouted.

Two of the bouncers escorted him toward the door. Ted and the other guy still had their arms wrapped around Draven until Brett was out of sight. Cashea glanced around at the thinning crowd. She guessed since there was to be no bar fight, they had lost interest.

"Are you cool?" Ted asked Draven who nodded.

Draven found Cashea. Her breath was

snatched from her lungs at the look in his eyes. His gaze did a once-over on her as if to make sure she was okay.

Ted released him and patted him on the shoulder. "What the fuck set you off?"

"That fucker doesn't know how to keep his hands to himself," Draven said. He jerked his chin toward Cashea. Ted glanced at her and raised his eyebrows. "He grabbed her."

"I'm sorry I didn't see it, Cashea," Ted said. Anger flooded his features. He ran a hand along his face. "If you want to press charges, just let me know."

"No, I'm good." She shook her head. All she wanted was for this to be over. She spun around and tried to find her water, but it was a lost cause. She and the girls only had a few more songs to go then they would be done for the night. After their set, the DJ would finish off the evening.

"Here ya go, doll. Don't worry about looking for the other one." Danny brought her another bottle. He slid it across the counter.

Cashea went over to the bar. Ted and Draven were speaking off to the side. She didn't know what they were saying, but it sure seemed as if Draven was reading Ted the riot act. The tension had yet to leave his body. His eyes were narrowed on Ted who stood nodding to whatever Draven was saying.

"Thanks, Danny," she murmured. She kept her head down and threaded her way through the crowd. She was sure the girls were wondering where she was. She arrived at the hallway where the dressing room was located and paused. She glanced over her shoulder and found Draven watching her. Her heart skipped a beat. She gave a little wave before continuing on her way.

Chapter Three

"Are you sure you are going to be okay?" Monica asked.

The girls stood around their makeshift dressing room. Their show was over, and they had returned to grab their things before leaving. They had been absolutely horrified to hear what Brett had done to her when she'd told them the story.

"I think I have pepper spray in my bag," Lilly announced. She yanked opened her oversized purse and began going through it. She grinned and held up her small device with pride.

"We won't need that." Cashea laughed. She stood from where she sat and grabbed her bag from the floor.

They had finished their set without any issues. With Ted tossing Brett out, Cashea didn't have to worry about him for the rest of the night. The crowd had danced and sung their hearts out with Cashea and the girls.

"You sure? I'm not afraid to use it." Lilly waved it around in a fake threat.

Giggles filled the room at her silly antics. Cashea was sure Lilly wouldn't have hesitated to use it on Brett had she had the chance. She was about the same height as Cashea and a spitfire.

"I just can't believe Brett thought he would be a match for Draven. That guy is so damn scary." Monica visibly shivered.

Murmurs went around. Sara, Kim, and Monica had all grown up in Ironhaven. Lilly and Cashea were the only two of the band who weren't from around here. Lilly had moved here a few years ago from Seattle. Her college friend and roommate were from Ironhaven and had talked her into moving to the small town.

Cashea held back a frown. She didn't think Draven looked scary. Hell, he had the brooding, silent "leave me the fuck alone" vibe just right. She didn't know why, but she thought it was damn sexy. She couldn't help it if she had a things for guys who were the silent type as well. She could talk enough for the both of them.

"Brett is used to everyone bowing down to him and his little friends," Sara said.

She opened the door and stepped out into the hallway with Monica and Lilly behind her. Lilly positioned herself against the door so it wouldn't close.

"It's about time someone stood up to him. You sure you won't want us to wait for you?" Sara asked.

"I'm good. I'm just going to change my shoes and be on my way. I'll see y'all on Monday after work." Cashea shooed them on. She didn't want to keep them any longer than necessary. It had been a long day for all of them. She'd gone to work earlier before coming out to the bar to perform. But she wasn't going to complain. Fridays in the office were light, and singing at the Hen House was for fun. If not for their band, Cashea was sure she'd be curled up on her couch with a good book, an old movie playing in the background, and a nice little drink.

"Be safe!" Monica called out.

Lilly gave a wave and moved out of the way so the door shut, leaving Cashea in their makeshift dressing room alone.

Cashea opened her bag and pulled her flip-flops

out. She wanted to take her cowboy boots off and switch over. She made quick work of slipping out of her boots and sliding her feet into the flops. She stuffed the boots into her bag before zipping it closed. She hefted the oversized bag up and placed the strap on her shoulder. She glanced around the room to ensure she and the girls weren't leaving anything behind. It wasn't anything fancy. There was a small couch, a couple of chairs, and a tiny bathroom. Along the wall was a long mirror for them to utilize with a vanity. The digs made them feel as if they were big superstars. Once in a while, the Hen House did host bands that came to Ironhaven.

Cashea shook her head and left the room and traveled down the hallway. The partying in the Hen House was in full swing. The DJ was playing a mix of hip-hop and country music. It worked for the eclectic crowd of young and older patrons. She made her way through the thick throng. There was always a rush of people who came out after midnight and filled the bar to the brim. Every now and then, Cashea and the girls hung out after their set, but tonight was not one of them. Everyone had plans except for her.

She had big plans to strip out of her clothes, which she was sure smelled like the bar, take a hot shower, throw on her jammies, and curl up on her couch with her blanket and find a good movie to watch.

Cashea's gaze found its way to the bar. Draven was still there. Her breath caught in her throat at the sight of him. The rest of their set, he hadn't turned back around. She'd paid attention to him to see if he would decide to watch her sing again, but he hadn't. She had felt slight disappointment but wasn't sure why. He never did, and now that he had once, what did she expect? Him to watch the entire show, clap and dance along with them?

She snorted at the notion.

She seriously doubted Draven danced, much less knew the songs she and the girls performed.

With a wave to Danny, she headed out of the Hen House. The night sky in South Dakota was absolutely breathtaking. It was dark and appeared as if someone had purposely painted the stars in their exact alignments. She stared up and inhaled the fresh air. One couldn't get this type of thing in the city. The short time she'd lived in the city, the sky just never seemed so clear, and the air wasn't as fresh. The entire time she'd lived in the city, she'd missed the small-town life.

Cashea held on to the strap of her bag while she made her way across the parking lot. Laughter rang out from a group of people congregating near a row of pickup trucks. She headed toward where her small SUV was parked. Her vehicle came into sight, and she frowned, pausing a few feet from it.

"What the hell?" she murmured. She stared at the white SUV. The back windshield had the word 'bitch' painted on it, and her poor truck leaned to one side. She scurried over to it, fear mounting inside her. She arrived at her truck and took in that both of the tires on the passenger side were slashed. Every ounce of air was gone from them. She bent down to assess the front one and saw a wicked gash in the rubber. "Are you fucking kidding me?"

She waved a hand in frustration and stood back up. No one seemed to be paying her any attention. It didn't take a rocket scientist to figure out who had done this to her truck.

Brett.

There couldn't be anyone else who would do this to her. She did a quick walk around her truck and didn't see anything broken off it. The doors were still locked. She unlocked them with her key fob and quickly jumped inside to make sure nothing was missing. Everything was still in place. Her spare change she left in the empty cup holder, her phone's charging cord, and even the pack of gum she'd left on the passenger seat.

"Just great," she groaned. She didn't get paid until next week and would not be able to cover the cost of a tow and two brand-new tires. She leaned her head back on the rest and blew out a frustrated breath. From what she remembered of what was in her bank account, she might be able to swing the tow and tires, but then that would mean no gas for the car and certainly no buying groceries until she got paid again.

She grabbed her pack of gum and tossed it into her bag and got out of her SUV. She locked the truck and headed back to the bar.

"Forget something?" Ted asked, stepping outside the bar. The bouncer stood by the door and folded his arms in front of his chest.

"Nope. Someone just decided to slash two of my tires," she announced with the fakest smile she could rustle up. Her anxiety level was through the roof. How could he do this to her? Just because she didn't want to go on a date with him? Was this supposed to make her change her mind? If he thought that, then he had another think coming.

"What?" He scowled. "Are you okay?"

"Oh, I'm just fine. It's not like I wanted to go home and chill. Now I need to call for a Uber and maybe I can get one in the next few hours," she grumbled.

"Here, let me call the police. We can file a report—"

"It's pointless, Ted," she said. It truly was. By the time the police came out it would probably be morning. In a small town on a weekend, if it wasn't an emergency, it was going to have to wait. A vandalized car was not top priority for the sheriff and deputies. Just like calling for an Uber. There weren't that many ridesharing drivers in their town, and for the ones who were operating, it would take them forever to arrive. She would call the police in the morning and file a report.

Ted opened the door for her. The muffled music blared at her as she walked back inside the bar. She pulled her phone out of her bag and blew out a deep breath. She headed over to the bar and found an empty seat near *him*. Her gaze landed on Draven who was still glued to the television.

That man sure did love him some football. A

new game was on. The only reason Cashea knew was because the players' uniforms were different colors.

"I thought you were leaving." Danny sidled up to her. He leaned his hands on the counter with concern in his eyes.

"I would have, but it would appear someone slashed my tires," Cashea drawled out. Her anxiety was quickly turning to anger. She wondered if the bar had any cameras out in the parking lot. If they had him on film doing it, then she could make him pay. Maybe get a lawyer and sue him.

She rolled her eyes. A lawyer? That would cost more than the damn tires. She was royally screwed in this matter. Who would believe her anyway? She was new to town, and Brett's family was well known. No one would believe her. They would probably spin it as if she were the one chasing him and using it as a stunt.

Yup, she was screwed.

"Say what now? You said your tires were slashed?" Danny sputtered. He dragged his fingers through his graying hair. He looked about as stressed as Cashea felt at the moment.

She slid her finger along the screen of her phone so she could open up the rideshare app.

"Are you sure?" he asked.

"Welp, if you want to go look yourself, then you'll see my truck with a major lean. Both of the passenger-side tires are completely flat," she said dryly. She punched in the information needed, and just what she'd thought, the cursor just circled and circled until it came back that no drivers were available. She sighed and opened up another rideshare app and repeated the information to see if they had cars. Of course there weren't any. She bit her lip and thought about texting Sara. She didn't live too far from Cashea. Maybe she wouldn't mind coming back to get her. "And the person even left me a message on my back windshield."

Cashea placed her phone on the counter. Draven pushed back from the bar abruptly. She jumped at the sudden move. Her eyes widened as he came to stand beside her.

"What did the message say?" Draven growled.

The scent of him washed over her. Even though they were in the bar, she picked up notes of sandalwood and musk. She tilted her head back to meet his gaze. Cashea swallowed hard, staring into his eyes. Maybe Monica was onto something. The glint in his eyes was definitely something dark.

"Bitch," she replied low. She didn't need to

speak up any louder. The way his nostrils flared told her that he'd heard her.

He reached in his back pocket and pulled his wallet out. He tossed a few bills toward Danny.

"Keep the change," he muttered. He turned back to her and jerked his head. "Let's go. I'll take you home."

Chapter Four

Draven wasn't sure when he'd taken hold of Cashea's wrist, but he told himself that it was so they didn't separate while walking through the crowd. Her soft skin was a direct contrast to the calluses that plagued his hand. He had the urge to want to run his hands along her entire body to see if the rest of her was just as silky smooth.

The Hen House was overly crowded tonight. It was no wonder Ted and his men hadn't seen Brett get handsy with Cashea. That shouldn't have gone down, and he'd made sure that Ted knew his thoughts about it.

Draven's anger rose again. He may not have

been looking at her when she'd returned to the bar, but he'd certainly known the instant she had arrived. He'd purposely continued to watch the game, but he'd heard every word she had said to Danny.

It would appear someone slashed my tires.

Draven had to control himself from getting up and going to find that asshole. The buzz he'd had from his drinks instantly disappeared. He already knew who had done this to her, and the fact that he'd left her a little message had Draven seeing red.

I should have broken something on that fucker, he growled in his head. It would look as if he would have to go and teach good ol' Brett some manners.

Draven was cut off by a guy trying to sweet talk some questionably young girl into something. Draven paused beside him, refusing to walk around him.

"Girl, my car is right out front," he said. He paused his begging and turned to Draven with a scowl. The guy tipped back his head and met Draven's glare. Whatever he was about to say froze on his lips.

"Move," Draven growled.

The guy didn't say a word but ushered the girl

out of the way. Draven continued on with Cashea in tow. They arrived at the entrance to the bar. He pulled her in front of him and pushed open the door to the bar to allow her to exit first. She dipped down slightly and went under his arm. He followed behind her and took in Ted standing outside.

"Were you able to find a ride?" Ted asked her.

She hefted her ridiculously large bag up on her shoulder. It looked too heavy for her. He didn't know what all she had in there.

"I'm her ride," Draven snapped. He moved over to her and took her hand in his. This time his cock stiffened. He bit back a curse. He shouldn't be having this type of reaction to her in front of another man. He glared at the bouncer and took a step closer to him. "How the hell did y'all allow that asshole to fuck with her car? What the fuck is the purpose of security here?"

"Whoa!" Ted held up his hands with his palms facing Draven. He took a step back from him. "Look, man, we can't be everywhere at once. I feel bad for Cashea. I offered to call the police."

"He did, but it's pointless," Cashea came to Ted's defense. She rested her free hand on his arm.

The move instantly calmed down his anger. He

blinked and looked at her. How the hell did she do that? He'd always had issues with anger and rage. He'd learned to utilize it when he was in the service, but never had anyone brought it under control with one touch.

"I just want to go home," she said. "I'll deal with it in the morning."

"Yeah. I'll put out a call and have an officer come out in the morning. I'll have them call you, Cashea," Ted replied. The bouncer focused on her.

Draven had yet to take his eyes off Ted. He didn't care what excuses the security guard came up with. It was no reason people couldn't come out and have a good time without being harassed or their vehicles damaged.

"See that you do." Draven didn't like the fact that Ted had Cashea's phone number. He glanced down at her. "Show me your car."

This time it was Cashea who led him. He reached over and took her damn bag from her. It was almost the same size as she was and just about as heavy.

"What the hell do you have in here?" he grumbled.

"Oh, I don't know. Work clothes, my boots, my

purse is stuffed in there, and some other things." She giggled.

The sound of her laugh had his heart skipping a beat. Draven frowned and was unused to these feelings he was getting while around her. He also noticed that she still held his hand. She could have let it go. It was a creep move, but he found himself hoping she didn't release him. Her hand felt damn good in his. She guided him to a small SUV parked not too far from his. He immediately saw the lean. He let go of her and walked to it.

He bent down and took in the deep gashes in her tires. The person had wanted to ensure that the tires wouldn't be able to be fixed but needed to be replaced. Draven stood and combed his fingers through his hair.

Brett was going to pay for this.

"I can't believe he did this. I mean, seriously. Women shoot down men all the time. Did he really need to do this?" Cashea sighed. She rested her hands on her waist. "This is going to cost me a fortune I can't afford right now."

"I'll take care of him." Draven wasn't going to let this slide. He took her by the hand again—still unsure why—and led her over to his truck.

"Why don't I like the way you said that?" she muttered.

He opened the passenger door and helped her in. He handed her the bag and shut the door. He walked around the back of his truck, his gaze going back to her little white SUV one more time, then he hopped inside his vehicle.

"Thanks for doing this. You don't have to," Cashea said. She reached for her safety belt and clicked in place.

Draven tried to not stare at her. She was fucking gorgeous with her light-brown skin, dark hair, and big brown eyes. Being inside the cab, he could smell her light perfume. His cock stiffened even more. He bit back a curse. He couldn't even remember the last time he'd been with a woman. Since coming home, women had been far from his mind.

"Don't worry about it." He hit the button to switch the truck on, guiding it through the parking lot. He paused at the mouth of the street and glanced at her. "Where do you live?"

She gave him quick instructions on how to get to her home. He pulled out onto the street and headed in that direction. The area she'd told him was a quiet residential location on the outskirts of town. They drove in silence for a few moments.

Cashea leaned forward and paused with her fingers on the radio.

"Do you mind?" she asked.

He shook his head. Music would help fill the silence. He certainly didn't know what to say to her. Now that she was in his truck, he was having a hard time concentrating. She smiled at him and turned on the radio. A classic rock station was on. She hopped around stations until she came to one she wanted.

"Is this okay?"

He tightened his grip on the steering wheel. She was just being friendly. Her smiles didn't mean anything.

At least that was what he was trying to convince his damn cock.

"Yeah. It's fine." He calculated how much time it would take them to get to the area she lived in. They should be there in about fifteen minutes.

Fuck.

Was he an ass for not starting a conversation? He sure as hell didn't know and normally he wouldn't care. But there was something about having Cashea near him. He thought quick, and before he knew it, the only thing that came to mind spilled from his lips.

"You do know you shouldn't get in the car with strangers, right?"

"Is that so?" Cashea's husky laugh filled the air. She shifted toward him and cocked her head to the side and studied him. "This is no different than me getting in an Uber. I don't know those people."

He focused on the road ahead of them. She was right, of course. He hadn't thought about it.

"At least they've had a background check."

She giggled again, and the sound went straight to his dick. He bit back a curse and had to keep himself from adjusting his damn bulge.

"But you aren't a stranger," she replied softly.

"You don't know nothing about me," he said gruffly. He slowed the truck down and eased onto a highway. The dark sky was littered with bright sparkling stars. He breathed in the fresh air coming in through the windows. With all of his deployments, he had missed glancing up at the sky at home. It just wasn't the same sky when he was in some damn bunker in a country that wanted him dead.

"I know plenty about you. Everyone talks about Draven Harvey."

He eyed her. What the hell was she talking

about? Who was everyone, and why was his name coming out of their mouths?

"Who?" His voice came out a bit too rough. He cleared his throat, not wanting to scare her. It was bad enough he had volunteered to take her home. He didn't trust anyone else to get her home safely at this time of night. All type of crazies came out when it got dark.

"I'm just playing with you." She grinned.

She reached up and tucked her dark hair behind her ear. The wind blowing in through their windows kept it flying around. Her perfume reached him again. He found himself breathing in the scent. It was soft and reminded him of her.

"You aren't as scary as people make you out to be," she said.

He glanced at her and decided to remain silent. She just didn't know what he was capable of. The music changed to a slow song. Cashea snapped her fingers to the beat and sang along with it. Her husky voice was smooth as silk. He had to admit she did have a lovely voice. He wondered if she had ever tried to sing professionally. She was that good. He'd heard plenty of people who thought they could sing but couldn't hold a note.

He allowed her voice to wash over him. Even

back in the bar, it was hard to not turn around to pay her attention. She deserved it. But every time he stared at her, it made him want things that he didn't deserve.

Cashea was a woman who deserved a man's last name.

Draven swallowed hard.

Cashea was a woman who he shouldn't even be thinking about touching. Hell, the things he wanted to do to her would probably have her running away. He glanced back over at her and found her swaying to the song as she sang. The wind had her skirt fluttering around, giving him a peek at her smooth thick thighs.

Fuck.

What he wouldn't give to have those soft thighs pressed against the sides of his head.

His grip tightened on the steering wheel again. He loosened his hands, not wanting to tear the damn thing off. They came to a red light. He brought his truck to a stop. He tried to think of everything but her thighs, her voice, the way those thin straps of her dress could easily be pushed aside.

Fuck.

Did she even have a bra on? From what he could see, he didn't think she did.

Now he was being a pervert. Draven swallowed hard and had to focus on the road once the light turned green.

"Are you happy to be back in town?" Her soft voice broke through his thoughts.

Draven turned to her and found her gaze on him. She slowly lowered her eyes and took him in before returning to his.

"Yeah." It was the honest truth. He could have settled anywhere once he retired, but he knew Ironhaven was for him. His family was here. His father had started something that Draven felt was important. Hell, he was one of the soldiers who needed Silver Creek. Who would have known when he'd left for the Marines that one day he would be someone needing help with being out of the service.

His father had been in the Navy, and it was his idea to buy the ranch and make it into what it had grown into. He was one honorable man, and Draven hoped to be half the man he was.

"I'm happy for you then," she said.

Another song came on, and they fell into a comfortable silence until she needed to give him the correct directions to her house. He pulled onto a quiet street. Draven recognized it. One of his buddies from high school used to live on the next street over.

He drove into her driveway and parked the truck.

"I really appreciate you bringing me home," Cashea said. She reached down for her heavy bag and brought it up onto her lap. She motioned to her house. "Want to come in for a nightcap?"

His gaze flicked to hers. He ran a hand along his face and stared at her. His brain was screaming no, while his cock was hollering yes.

"Cashea..."

"Just one drink. At least let me thank you properly. If not a drink, then maybe something else. I made a cake yesterday. Let me give you a piece. I made it from scratch." She tilted her head to the side to study him.

Even in the low light, Draven saw there was more than drinks and cake being offered. Her lips were curled up into a sexy grin.

Should he take her up on it? He couldn't offer much but one hell of a night.

His gaze fell to her shoulder where one of those damn straps slipped off to the side.

"Sure. Cake sounds good."

"Great!" Her grin widened.

He cut the engine and slipped out of the truck. He walked around the front of the vehicle and came to her door. He opened it and helped her down. Her body brushed his on the way down. She was trapped between him and the truck. He softly shut the door, not wanting it to slam. She tilted her head back to meet his gaze. He stood about six three while the top of her head barely came to his mid chest.

"Do you like chocolate?" Cashea asked. There was an upward tilt to the way she asked her question.

Her husky voice sent a electric bolt of lightning through Draven. He didn't step back away from her. He knew he should have, but he liked the feeling of her soft body pressed against his. His life for the past few years had been filled with the harshness of reality most civilians would never know about. He needed to touch her. Feel her. His eyes were drawn to her full lips.

He swallowed hard from the images of them wrapped around his cock. Fuck. She'd asked him a question. Her head was tilted to her side as she waited for his answer. Did he like chocolate? The image of her thighs floated back to the forefront of his mind.

"I do."

Cashea's lips curled up into her sexy grin. She took his hand in hers and guided him toward her house. The sway of her hips was mesmerizing. She looked over her shoulder at him as if to make sure he hadn't disappeared.

Draven wasn't going anywhere but wherever she was leading him.

Chapter Five

Cashea would be the first to admit she had lost all of her marbles. She'd never propositioned a guy who she had just met for sex. Draven was the epitome of sexiness, and she wanted him. There was nothing wrong with a woman going after a man she desired. In this day and age, a woman could do what and who she pleased.

And right now, she wanted Draven.

She hadn't lied to him. She had baked a cake from scratch yesterday, but she couldn't help but tease him a little and ask if he liked chocolate. She bit back a giggle knowing that had been her sneaky little way of asking if he liked Black women. The way his eyes had narrowed on her, he knew exactly what she was asking.

And his answer didn't disappoint.

His large hand engulfed hers as she led them up the few steps to her home. She paused in front of the door and remembered she needed to get her keys. She bit back a groan at the feel of his body pressing against hers. It was hard and toned in all of the right places.

Lord, help me.

Cashea bit her lip and reached into her bag to search for her house keys. She didn't want to release his hand. He might come to his senses and change his mind.

"You need some help?" Draven's deep voice broke through her thoughts.

Her fingers connected with her keychain. She pulled it out and held them up. She spun around and grinned.

"Nope. Found them." She turned back to the door and slipped her key in. She pushed open the door and was thankful she'd remembered to leave her lamp on in the living room. "Welcome to my home."

She stepped inside and finally let his hand go.

Draven followed behind her and closed the door. Cashea didn't miss the sound of the lock engaging. Now that he was in her home, there was a flutter of butterflies deep in her belly. She kicked her shoes off and waved for him to go with her down the short hallway. He toed off his boots and strolled behind her.

"You have a nice home," he drawled.

They entered the living room, and for once she was glad she hadn't left her normal mess of blankets, books, and stuff in there.

"Thanks. I rent it. I moved here a year ago and wasn't sure if I would be staying or not." She shrugged. She tossed her bag on the floor beside the couch. She loved her landlady. Miss Daphne was a sweet older woman who was retired and owned two properties that helped bring in additional income for her. The home was a ranch-style property with two bedrooms and one bath. It was the perfect size for her. "Here, let me get you that cake I promised."

She spun on her heel and scurried to the kitchen.

No need to get scared now, girl.

She bit back a chuckle. She flipped on the light in the kitchen and beelined it to the sink. She had fallen in love with the kitchen when she'd first seen it. She loved to cook and bake, and it had plenty of room for her to do everything she would need to do. After washing her hands, she obtained two plates and utensils. Her prized cake she'd baked was on the island safely secured under a glass dome. She lifted the top and was assaulted by the aroma of sweet chocolatey goodness. Footsteps echoed behind her. She looked over her shoulder to find Draven standing in the doorway.

Her breath caught in her throat at the sight of him practically filling up the space. The room suddenly felt too small. Her heart raced as she met his light-blue eyes which were locked on her. The heat in them had her clenching her thighs together. Her gaze traveled down to his shirt that was causally draped over his muscular body that she'd got to feel for a brief moment. Her gaze dropped down to the area she had felt a very large bulge and wondered what his dick looked like.

She snapped her gaze away and turned back to the cake. She cut him a piece and placed it on a plate.

"One piece of cake for you," she announced.

He came to her side and leaned against the island. The warmth of his gaze did not leave her. Cashea's skin prickled as if he had already touched her. She grabbed a fork and presented the cake to him. She sliced a piece and held the fork out to him. He glanced down at it first before coming back to meet her stare. He opened his mouth slightly and allowed her to feed him the first bite.

The fluttering in her stomach increased. Draven slowly chewed then swallowed. She placed the plate down on the counter and closed the short distance between them. She needed to touch him again. His hands came to rest on her waist automatically. Her hands rested on his solid wall of a chest. She tilted back her head so she could watch his expression.

"What do you think?" she breathed. Her hands slowly traveled up, and she pressed closer. Her breasts were crushed between them. His body radiated a heat and power that she could feel coiled up inside him.

His eyes darkened as they watched her.

"It's good," he murmured.

She leaned up on her tiptoes, and his head lowered. Their lips met in a hard kiss. Draven's tongue thrust inside her mouth, immediately dominating the kiss. The taste of the chocolate greeted her. A moan left her; his hands moved down to her ass and brought her flush against him. Cashea's fingers made their way to his head and dove into his thick hair.

The power of his kiss washed over her. His lips were soft and steady as they moved along hers. His tongue baited hers, sweeping inside to coax hers to duel with his. Cashea tilted her head to the side, the kiss deepening. Draven spun them around to where her back met the island. His lips left hers and blazed a hot trail of kisses along her jawline and down to her neck. His callused hand slid along her shoulders, knocking the thin straps of her dress down her arms. She shimmied them and allowed the dress to fall to her feet.

Draven paused and lifted his head. Her hands slipped from him and came to rest on the island behind her. She bit her lip, his heated gaze sweeping along her. Usually, this would be the moment all of her insecurities came rushing to her, but they weren't there. Her body wasn't perfect. It wasn't model thin. She had hips, she had a pudge of a stomach, large breasts, and ample ass. With the way Draven was hungrily staring at her, she felt downright sexy.

She dragged air into her lungs and wondered what he was thinking. Her nipples pressed against her strapless bra. The irritating material had to go.

She reached up and unsnapped the contraption and let it fall to the floor with her dress, leaving her only in her small scrap of panties.

"Fuck," Draven cursed. His gaze flicked to hers. The hunger burned bright in his blue orbs. His hands came to rest on her cheeks. "Are you sure, Cashea?"

She reached for the bottom of his shirt, dying to see what he looked like underneath it. She jerked her head in a nod, unable to formulate words. She tugged on the cotton material and dragged it over his head. She dropped it down onto the growing pile of clothes. Her hands returned to him and softly traced the lines on his stomach. He was like chiseled marble. Smooth skin, muscles well defined, and a sprinkle of hair on his chest that trailed down his abdomen and disappeared beneath his jeans. Absolutely breathtaking.

"My bedroom is down the hall," she whispered, finally getting her voice back.

He bent down and hoisted her up by the backs of her knees. She held on to him and wrapped her legs around his waist. He spun around and exited the kitchen and made his way down the hall. They burst through her bedroom door. She had left the small lamp on her nightstand on since she had known she would return home late.

Draven stalked his way to her bed. He gently placed her on the center then stood back. She lifted onto her elbows and watched him reach for his belt. Her breaths were coming a mile a minute. He slid the belt open then reached for the button of his jeans. This was one show Cashea could not look away from. He pushed down his jeans, revealing his black boxer briefs. Her gaze zeroed in on the large bulge that was pressing against the cotton material. He knelt on the bed and came to her. He braced himself over her and lowered his head.

He paused; his lips mere millimeters from hers. Those eyes of his had her captivated. They grew darker as they took her in.

"Cashea, I can't offer much," he began.

She reached up and pressed her finger to his lips. He didn't need to go any further. She wasn't asking for anything from him. There was no reason he needed to think she would want something from him after this night. They were two consenting adults who needed what the other could provide. There was something in his eyes that revealed he needed this.

She could be the reprieve of whatever demons were on his shoulders.

"How about just tonight?" she whispered. She cupped his face and brought him down to seal their lips together.

He froze for a brief moment before opening his mouth. The kiss quickly grew frantic. Cashea gave him a push, and Draven fell back onto his back. She smiled and knelt on the bed. His eyes didn't leave her when she hooked her fingers underneath her panties and pulled them down.

She tossed them over onto the floor. "Let me take care of you."

Her hands went to his shoulders. She leaned over him and softly kissed him. She had a deep desire to make him feel wanted and needed. She had a feeling his life hadn't been easy, and if she could give him one night where he could let go of everything that was on his mind, then she would be one happy woman.

One of his hands cupped the back of her head while their kiss deepened. She moaned, loving the feeling of her naked body resting next to his. She broke the kiss and trailed her lips over the rough shadow of a beard he had. The short bristles tickled her nose. She trailed kisses along his chin and dove down to his chest. There was something about a man with a chiseled chest that did it for her. Draven was a man who worked the land and was in top shape. She was sure most of it was from his time in the service, but now that he was no longer, he still apparently kept himself in top shape. Her tongue slid down to his erect nipples. She bathed both of them, then traveled down to the ridges of his abdomen.

Cashea glanced up and caught Draven staring at her. She offered a little smirk. Her hands went to band of his underwear. She couldn't wait to unwrap him. His cock tented the cotton material. He lifted his hips to help her. She tugged on the drawers until she freed his hard member.

"Hmmm..." a guttural groan escaped Cashea. She'd felt that he was large, but holy mother...she hadn't expected this.

"What is it?" He grunted.

They worked to take his underwear off. Her gaze flicked back to the monster before going to meet his hooded eyes.

"Um, nothing," she murmured.

She roved her hands over his muscular thighs and made her way back to his cock. She wrapped her hand around it and took in the warmth of his shaft. It was thick and long with a vein running up the underside of it. The mushroom tip was angry-looking and darker than the rest of the length of him. Her hand slid up him, then going down to the base. She smirked at him, feeling her humor coming through.

"Just admiring this."

"Is that so?" He arched an eyebrow at her. He propped himself up on his elbows.

"Yup." She lowered her head and snuck her tongue out to tease the tip of his cock.

He narrowed his eyes on her. She held his gaze while she repeated her action again. His quick intake of breath was his only response. She opened her mouth and drew him inside it. She was determined to worship his cock for a long time.

Cashea took her time. She pushed herself to take as much as she could. She was going to put all of her skills to the test. Her hand slipped along him. Her saliva providing slipperiness for her. She gripped him while she hollowed out her cheeks.

A moan and curse burst from his lips. Her core clenched. There was nothing sexier than hearing a man moan from pleasure. She tightened her hold on him and sucked him harder and farther into her mouth. His fingers entwined in her hair. Her eyes fluttered closed from the sensation that shot through her body. Her pussy was drenched with need. She didn't mind one bit about his fingers holding on to her hair. Cashea bit back a giggle. He was just lucky she wasn't wearing one of her glueless wigs tonight.

"Fuck. Cashea," he groaned.

She increased her pace on him. Her hands glided in tandem with her mouth. She couldn't fit the entire length of him inside so she utilized her hands to make up for it. His grip tightened more, and she kept going. She wanted to see him let loose. He didn't appear to be a man who lost control often.

Draven's hips thrust upward, sinking his cock farther into her mouth.

Her thighs were coated in her juices. She couldn't wait to feel this cock push inside her. It had been a long time since she'd been intimate with anyone. Her last boyfriend had been mediocre in bed. The only reason she'd stayed with him so long was because he was nice.

But nice didn't give her world-shattering orgasms.

She used her free hand and cupped his scrotum. She massaged it and felt the tension spread through his muscles.

"Cashea," he gasped.

He pulled his cock from her mouth. Their panting filled the air. He shook his head, his eyes electric. She smirked and crawled up over him. She tossed a leg over him and straddled him. His cock nestled between her thighs. She groaned at the feeling of his hard length brushing her clit.

"I wasn't done yet." She pouted.

She rested her hands on either side of his head. She shifted her hips and dragged her pussy along the length of him. It felt so damn good, she did it again.

"Yes, the hell you were," he growled.

He clutched her hip with one hand while the other one covered her breast. Her mound filled his hand completely. He brought it down to his mouth and nipped her beaded bud. She gasped from the slight pain. He bathed the nipple with his tongue, suckling it inside his mouth. She ground her pussy down on his length again so she could rub her clit against him. She fisted the blanket tight. Her soft moans grew louder as she rocked back and forth.

"Draven," she gasped.

"Lift up," he ordered.

She didn't hesitate to do as he'd commanded. He guided the blunt tip of his cock to her slippery opening. She lowered herself with a deep groan expelling from her. His cock spread her wide and invaded her snug sheath. Her walls burned from the stretching of his girth. She sank down farther on him until he was fully submerged inside her.

"Oh, fuck," she breathed.

She had never felt so full in her life. Her head was thrown back, and she rested her hands on his stomach. She had to wait until she grew accustomed to his invasion. She rocked her hips, and another moan was ripped from her. Cashea inhaled and opened her eyes and found Draven watching her. She squeezed her muscles around him, eliciting a moan from him.

She rose then sank back down on him. Her swollen clit rubbed against his length. She did it again and again. Her moans grew louder. Draven thrust his hips, sending his cock deeper.

Together they set a steady rhythm. Every movement brought a ripple of pleasure through her body. Her pussy grew impossibly wetter, and she continued her actions.

"That's right, Cashea," he murmured.

She fell forward, resting her hands on the bed beside his head. He gripped her waist and took over. The room filled with the sounds of their copulation, her slickness making itself known. She wasn't even embarrassed about the amount of noise her pussy was making. His length slipped in and out of her with no issue. He bucked his hips while holding her in place. He fucked her harder, and she welcomed it.

"Yes," she hissed.

Her body trembled. Each thrust of his hips sent his cock deep, and her clit stimulated. She squeezed her eyes tight, her orgasm racing toward her. Draven pounded into her and sent her barreling to the stars.

A scream erupted from her lips. "Draven!"

His grunts joined her, and he bellowed his release. Warmth flooded inside her. She shook uncontrollably, her climax washing over her. She fell forward, no longer able to hold her own weight. He caught her, wrapping his arms around her. Cashea's face was nestled in the crook of his neck. Her breaths were coming so fast she couldn't control them. Their bodies were slick with sweat. His warm, hard body felt good underneath her. His cock stayed nestled inside her.

At the moment, she couldn't move if she needed to, but in all honesty, she didn't want to.

Chapter Six

Draven guided his truck up the driveway of his home and parked it in front of the garage. He killed the engine and blew out a deep breath. He glanced over at the clock and saw that it was a little after six in the morning. He ran a hand along his face. He was late for work. He was supposed to report in at five-fifteen. It may be Saturday, but there was always work that needed to be done on a ranch.

Draven leaned his head back against the headrest, not even bothered that he was just arriving home.

How about just tonight? Cashea's voice echoed in his head. It was like she had known what he was about to say before it even left his lips. The memory of her soft skin over his had his cock hardening all over again. He hadn't wanted to leave her bed, but he had to. There was nothing he could offer her.

Their night together had been mind-blowing. Her pussy had fit around him like a glove. She had tasted like the sweetest peach he'd ever had the pleasure to eat. He could still taste her delicious cunt on his tongue now. Her cries of pleasure still rang out in his ears. He closed his eyes and could still see her smooth brown skin as he had run a hand over her thick thighs.

He opened his eyes and tried to push the memory of Cashea's cries from his memory. That's all it was going to be now. He'd slipped from her bed while she'd slept and snuck out of her house. It hadn't sat right with him for some reason. It wasn't the first time he'd had one night with a woman, but for some reason, sneaking out this time left a bad taste in his mouth.

"Get moving, Harvey," he muttered.

He opened the door to his truck and stepped out of it. He went into the house and made his way to his bedroom. He stripped off his clothing and hopped in the shower. The stinging hot water poured over him. He turned his back toward the jets and bit back a curse. A slight pain appeared on his right shoulder. He reached out a hand and ran his fingers over the area. The memory of Cashea's nails scraping and digging into his shoulder surfaced. She might be all smiles and sexiness, but the woman sure was a hellcat in bed.

He wasn't sure how, but he was going to have to put her out of his mind. There wasn't going to be a future for them, so he needed to move on.

Maybe even start going to one of the other bars in town. Cashea sang with her band at the Hen House every week. Hell, they had the best beer on tap, and Danny's service was superb.

He was fucking screwed.

Draven snatched his soap up and washed up. He didn't take long in the shower. He was sure his father was going to be wondering where he was. They had plenty of work to do today. They were supposed to be moving one of the herds to the southern pasture, but he was going to have to be a little later than usual. He had some business to take care of. His father would understand. In the year he'd been back on the ranch, he'd never been late nor had he missed a day.

Twenty minutes later, he strolled out of his house and jogged down the stairs. He hadn't had any caffeine yet. He'd grab some over at the main house. He was sure Miss Bee had her signature brew waiting. He jumped back in his truck and headed over to where his father lived.

Miss Bee was a pretty woman in her late fifties who had been hired to work for his father after his wife had passed. Miss Bee was in charge of cleaning and cooking. She even cooked for the ranch hands. Her meals were legendary. Her desserts were one of a kind. Even when Draven was in the service he would receive packages from Miss Bee. She'd always toss in a letter and put 'from Andy and Bee.' Her peanut butter cookies were one of his favorites. When he was stateside, he looked forward to receiving a box from her.

That woman was sure sweet on his father. Draven hadn't asked him if there was something going on between the two of them. He wasn't sure even at his age if he wanted to know certain things about his father.

The Silver Creek Ranch was a large enough stead that his father had gifted Draven and his brother land and had even built homes for them on it. The ranch was to be their legacy, and when Draven had first come home, he hadn't felt like staying in his home alone. They had built the house a few years back when he had first mentioned retiring. His father wanted to ensure that each of his sons had a place of their own. His brother, Ridge's home, wasn't that far from Draven's. They had their own little corners of the ranch where they could have privacy.

If Andy had his way, both Ridge and Draven would settle down, get married, and start their own families right here on the ranch. Draven snorted. Maybe Ridge was willing to settle down. His brother was good-looking and outgoing. Some lucky woman was out there waiting on him. He was crazy intelligent, too. He'd gone to college and became a veterinarian. Their father utilized him as the local vet for all of the animals on the ranch, which was handy since Ridge lived on the Silver Creek property.

Draven parked his truck out front of the main house. It still looked the same as it had when he was a young kid. The house had seemed massive when he was younger. There were lots of good memories in this home. Ridge and he had been lucky. Their childhood was filled with love and laughter. Draven caught sight of himself in the rearview mirror and stared.

What had happened to him?

War, that's what happened.

He killed the engine and got out of his truck. He walked up to the front door and tapped on the screen door a couple of times before opening it. One thing about his father's house, the front door was never locked.

"Pops?" he called out.

Andy didn't answer. He figured his father would be out on the ranch somewhere. Draven pulled his phone out of his jean pocket and sent a text to his father's lead ranch hand, Buck, to let him know he was not coming in to work this morning. At first he was just going to be late, but he'd decided he would take the entire day off. He slipped his phone back into his pocket and headed to the kitchen. The aroma of freshly brewed coffee assaulted him.

"Draven, is that you?" a singsong voice called out.

He arrived to the kitchen and found Miss Bee standing by the stove. The kitchen had recently been renovated a few years back. She had complained to his father that she needed a kitchen that was up to date in this century. Miss Bee, or Belinda Butler, was a robust woman with a huge personality. Her warm brown skin practically glowed.

She smiled, and two dimples were revealed. "How are you this morning?"

"I'm good, Miss Bee," he replied. Draven paused and thought about how he really felt, and it was true. The couple of hours he'd slept at Cashea's was the best sleep he'd gotten in years. He walked over to the counter where the freshly brewed coffee sat.

Bee moved around to the cabinet and snagged him a traveling mug with the ranch's logo on it.

"Really? That's good to hear." She handed him the filled mug then moved back over to stove.

Draven took a sip of the coffee and exhaled. It was as he'd expected. Miss Bee had a secret ingredient she claimed to put in the coffee that made it addictive.

"Do you have a minute or are you headed back out on the ranch?" she asked.

"I actually have to go into town for something," he replied. He leaned back against the counter and took another sip.

She turned around, and it was then he saw she was in the midst of plating freshly baked muffins. His mouth immediately watered.

"How about I just fix one of these to go for

you?" She arched an eyebrow at him and waited for his response.

"Yes, ma'am." He moved over toward her so he could see what kind of muffins they were.

She chuckled and placed the plate on the island. He inhaled and was greeted with the sweet smell of bananas. Draven had a weakness for banana muffins. She even had walnuts on top of them. His stomach rumbled from the aromas in the kitchen.

"I'll take two, please."

"But of course, dear."

Draven may have business to handle in town, but he would wait for these muffins. He'd eat them in the truck.

She rushed around the kitchen and wrapped his muffins up and placed them in a small paper bag. "If you are looking for Andy, he's out back."

"Thank you," Draven took the bag from her and tipped his head to her. He spun on his heel and headed toward the door that led to the back porch. He stopped at the door and thought of something. He hadn't really spoke with Bee lately. She was a staple on the ranch, and he should make time for her. He paused and turned back to her. "Um, are your girls doing well?"

Bee's face lit up at the question. Draven almost felt ashamed that he didn't sit down with her more and have conversations. His brother had breakfast with her and their father often, but Draven never really joined them. Ridge always got on him about his anti-social personality, but since coming home, he'd just wanted to be left alone. He wouldn't make good company and was told he could be very blunt and insensitive at times.

"They are doing fabulous, honey. I thank you for asking." Her smile was wide as she watched him. Bee's daughters were grown and in their early thir-ties. He'd met them once when they had come to visit and he'd been home on leave. "If you get hungry tonight, stop by and pick you up a plate, okay?"

"Yes, ma'am," he drawled. Maybe he would call his brother and see what he was doing and tell him to come over to the house, too. It would be good to spend quality time with the old man and his brother. Bee was a sweet woman, and he didn't mind being around her. He headed out the door. He stepped out on the porch and took in his father walking back to the house. He went down the stairs to meet him halfway.

"Morning," Andy called out. The older man

took his time walking across the yard toward the house. His stark gray hair looked slightly wet, and the ends were curling up. "I see someone didn't get home until early this morning."

"Hey, Pops." Draven ignored his father's observation. He wasn't going to get into where he had been. If he told him he had been with a woman, the old man might start making assumptions that Draven was involved with someone. Cashea's face came to mind. The way her features softened when she'd smiled at him while they'd lain together in the bed. Her smile had been the last thing he'd seen before he'd drifted off to sleep. He loosened his grip on his bag, not wanting to tear it apart and risk losing his muffins to the ground. He lifted his mug to his lips again.

"I hear you aren't coming to work today." Andy reached him and came over by him and gave him a firm pat on the back. He had always been a caring father who Draven and Ridge could turn to. He ensured his boys never wanted for anything, financially, mentally, or physically. "Everything all right?"

"I have some things I need to handle in town." Draven shrugged. There was something he had to take care of that wouldn't be able to wait long. The aroma of Bee's banana muffins was summoning him. He couldn't wait to dive into them. He was sure they were still warm, moist, and buttery. That woman had a gift, and the ranch was lucky to have her.

"Well, your message sent Buck in a tizzy. You know he hates technology and the text messaging." His father chuckled. He nodded toward Draven's hand. "I see you've visited with Bee."

"Yeah, I needed some coffee." Draven took another sip. He started to feel guilty about dipping out on them. Maybe he should hurry back and saddle up to help out. "When I get back, if y'all still are out there, I'll come and join you."

"Don't worry about it. We'll be fine. There are good men working this ranch. This is the small herd. It shouldn't take too long out there. I was just coming to the house. I left my darn phone. I need to call your brother and have him come check on one of the calves." Andy ran a hand along his face and eyed Draven. "You sure everything is okay?"

"Pops, I promise I'm good. I'm just going to town to go to the hardware shop."

"For what? What's wrong up at your house? Need me to come take a look?"

Draven allowed a small smile to come forward.

He shook his head and backed away from his father. Andy had always been a man who was good with his hands. Draven's mother used to call him Mister Fix-it. Draven's heart softened at the thought of his mother. She had been beautiful, soft-spoken, and kind. She was taken from them way too damn soon. He missed her something fierce. He never understood how someone so kind and loving could be burdened with something as vicious as cancer.

"Nope. Just have a certain hardware store owner I need to go have a chat with." Draven gave a little wave and made his way around the house to the front where he'd parked his truck. He just hoped the owner of the hardware store was in today. They needed to have a conversation. Apparently, he hadn't got the message last night at the Hen House.

Brett Falco was going to pay for Cashea's tires.

Draven tipped back the travel mug and finished off the rest of his coffee. He set the empty container down in the cupholder and waited. The muffins Bee had given him had not survived the ride into town. The woman had a talent that was not wasted. They had been everything Draven had known they would be. He glanced over at the crumpled bag resting on the passenger seat and wished he'd asked for three of them.

He had arrived in town and had parked outside Iron Hardware. It was owned by Brett's family and had been for years. It was one of two major hardware stores in Ironhaven. Draven tapped his fingers on the steering wheel while his gaze was locked on the front door of the store.

Iron Hardware was located in a small plaza with a few other stores. It was early in the morning, and most of the shops were just now opening. A few pedestrians were ambling down the street. Draven was sure traffic would pick up soon as the day went by. Hopefully, he wouldn't have to wait long for Brett to show.

Draven glanced in his driver's-side rearview mirror and took in a large silver pickup truck parking in a handicap spot. Music blared loudly from the vehicle before it suddenly cut off. Draven's interest was piqued. He was sure whoever was driving the vehicle didn't need that spot. Draven stiffened when he saw who was getting out of the driver's door.

Brett.

Looked as if Draven was going to get his wish

and not have to be here all morning waiting for the dipshit to show. He slid his keys into his pocket and stepped from his truck. He grabbed his brimmed hat and slammed it down on his head. He shut his door and headed toward the silver truck. Brett had yet to see him. He'd walked to the rear of his truck and was getting something out of the back.

"It's a fine morning, isn't it." Draven slowly strolled alongside the silver vehicle. It was an over-sized cab and top-of-the-line. It must have cost Brett a pretty penny. New tires for Cashea's car shouldn't be a problem for him.

"What the fuck do you want?" Brett glanced over at him. His eyes narrowed in on Draven. He pulled a duffle bag from the back of the truck and hefted the straps to rest on his shoulder.

"It would seem that we are not done with our little conversation we had last night." Draven folded his arms over his chest. He didn't like the man in front of him. He knew what type of guy Brett was. He was a user and an abuser. He was a decent-looking guy, and in small towns that meant he would think he was God's gift to women. Draven had met plenty of men like him. They were all the same. It was no wonder he hadn't taken Cashea's rejections lightly. He was used to getting everything he wanted.

"Oh, we are done all right. Don't think you can come bully me. I'll call the fucking police." Brett spun on his heels and walked to the other side of the truck.

Draven smirked and walked around the hood, meeting him on the sidewalk. Draven had no problems using his size to intimidate the other man. Brett sure had no problems putting his hands on women who didn't ask for it. The memory of Cashea's slashed tires came to mind.

"I don't think we are. Someone slashed Cashea's tires last night." Draven took another step toward Brett who backed up.

"Sounds like she has bad fucking luck," Brett snapped.

"Or maybe some son of a bitch, who doesn't understand the word no, took a knife to them." Draven closed the gap between them. If he had to beat the money out of Brett, he would. He would pay for the damage to Cashea's car. It had been a dick move.

"And you think I did it?" Brett smirked.

"Oh, I'm sure you did it," Draven growled.

"You don't have any proof, old man," Brett spat. "That bitch deserved it, too."

Draven saw red. He snatched Brett up by his shirt and slammed him into the side of his truck. The vehicle rocked from the force of Brett's body. His bag slid down to the ground, forgotten.

"Don't call her a bitch," Draven warned. His fist ached to wipe that smirk clean off Brett's face.

Brett had the audacity to laugh. "Why not? You want her for yourself? She's a fucking tease. Her pussy's probably no good any-damn-way."

Brett tried to push Draven off him but failed. Draven was close to losing his shit and pummeling Brett's face. He had no right to speak of Cashea in that manner. She was a good woman with a big heart. Her smile had brought out feelings he had thought were long gone. Memories of sinking into her warm cocoon had Draven wanting to defend her against everything. Brett didn't deserve a woman like Cashea, much less even be able to say her name.

"You're going to pay for her tires, asshole," Draven bit out through clenched teeth.

"Who the fuck is going to make me?"

Draven landed an short jab into Brett's stomach. He folded over immediately, gasping for breath. Draven bit back a grin. It had felt good. He'd purposely hit him right in the gut. He was surprised the idiot hadn't tossed whatever he'd had for breakfast.

"Is everything all right between you two?" an older gentleman asked, standing inside the doorway of the drugstore that was located next to the hardware store.

"Everything is fine," Draven replied.

He released Brett who fell to the ground on his hands and knees. His loud wheezing filled the air. The man eyed Brett then flicked his gaze back to Draven.

"Just a little misunderstanding," Draven said.

"We don't want any trouble around here, so you boys take your misunderstanding elsewhere."

"Yes, sir." Draven gave a short nod to the elderly man. He grabbed Brett by the arm and forced him up to his feet.

Brett inhaled sharply and glared at Draven. He rested back on his truck, taking deep breaths. Draven took a step back away from him and held his hands up. The older guy stood there for a moment before he went back inside the store.

Draven waited a moment then turned back to Brett. "Replace her tires."

"You can go fuck yourself," Brett snapped.

Draven moved toward him, but Brett scrambled out of his reach and ran to the other side of his truck. He held a hand to his stomach while he continued to struggle to breathe. There was a small gathering across the street, watching. Draven bit back a growl. He rested his hands on his waist and glanced around. Just that quick he had forgotten they were out in public.

Draven's gaze landed on a sheriff's patrol car sitting at the red light at the corner. The light switched to green, and the cruiser turned the corner and headed their way. Draven stood where he was and folded his arms. He watched the car approach, waiting to see if Brett would flag the deputy down. It slowed for a moment then continued on. Draven glared at Brett and pointed at him.

"Don't make me find you again." He walked around the front of Brett's truck and entered the street.

Brett quickly moved back to the sidewalk. Draven smirked and headed to his truck. He just hoped the fucker heeded his warning. Next time, he wasn't going to be so nice.

Chapter Seven

"It's going to cost *how* much?" Cashea groaned.

Her head dropped into her hand as she listened to the man on the phone rattle off pricing for replacing her tires. She squeezed her eyes shut, praying that she was still back home in her bed, dreaming. It was bright and early. She was in the office, which was surprisingly slow for a Monday morning. Usually, Dr. Reddy's office would be bustling with parents bringing in their children for their doctor's appointments. Maybe it was because it was the summer and families were spending more time together and vacationing. Cashea wasn't sure what the reason was, but she was thankful for the small break. Come fall, there would be an abundance of appointments and kids being brought in with new sniffles and more.

"Miss Moss, we do have an option of a credit company that would help you with the expenses. I can give you that information to read if you want," Hal, the mechanic, said.

Cashea sighed. She didn't need any more credit cards at the moment. She had proudly paid off all of her debts and tried to only use them when absolutely necessary. Welp, walking to work this morning proved that it was necessary. She had even had to pay for her car to be towed to his shop.

Another expense she couldn't afford.

"Let me look into some things," she said. She lifted her head and tucked her thick hair behind her ear. She would stall just a few more hours if need be. It seemed as if she would be running at least one of her cards back up.

"Oh, sure. You know how to reach me, dear," the older gentleman said.

She ended the conversation with the promise to call him by the end of the day. She sat back in her chair and glanced out into the waiting room. Only two patients so far. She'd already gotten them checked in for Dr. Reddy.

"Everything all right?" Tiffany asked from behind Cashea.

She turned to see Dr. Reddy's nurse leaning against the wall. Cashea stood from her desk and moved the bell to the counter in case someone else came into the office. She motioned to Tiffany to follow her toward the hall. Tiffany had welcomed Cashea immediately when she'd first begun working for the pediatrician. The medical crew had been sharing the duty of receptionist until they'd hired someone.

"Yeah and no," Cashea said. She leaned back against the wall and ran a hand along her face. "Let's just say Hal can give me new tires and get my car ready for me today, but I'd have to basically give him my firstborn."

"Ouch, that bad?" Tiffany reached out and rubbed Cashea's shoulder. Her big brown eyes were full of compassion. Her deep-brown skin glowed against her blonde-and-brown braids she had pulled back away from her face. She was one of the first people to help introduce Cashea around, and that's how she'd met Sara, Tiff's best friend. She'd heard Cashea singing one day in the back while she'd made copies of patient education materials and had told her that her friend was hoping to start up a cover band.

"Yeah. I'll be breaking out the credit card to pay for this."

"Insurance won't pay?"

Cashea winced. She had chosen the cheapest coverage she could get away with. Now she certainly regretted it, but who would have known she would have to replace two tires because an asshole couldn't deal with rejection from a woman?

"I have a high deductible and might as well just pay for the damn things."

"Why don't you file a police report? Make him pay for what he did to your car. That's not fair. You shouldn't be dealing with this." Tiffany scowled. She folded her arms.

"It's my word against his, and who is going to believe me over someone like him?" Cashea shook her head. She might as well chalk it up as a loss and cough up the money. Even a year later, she was still the new girl in town while Brett's family had been in Ironhaven for generations.

"Someone needs to stand up to him. He's just an ass for no reason." Tiff sighed.

Cashea had shared with Tiff what had happened between her and Brett this weekend.

Cashea had spoken with Tim earlier, and he'd reviewed the tapes from the security cameras. There was no footage of Brett slashing her tires, so she had no proof to even try to press charges against him.

Cashea bit her lip at the thought of the one person who hadn't had any issues standing up to Brett.

Draven.

Her heart raced with the thought of those almost iridescent blue eyes of his. Her skin prickled with the memory of his hands running along her thighs. They had been rough and callused, a direct contrast to her skin. A shiver passed through her. The orgasms he'd wrung from her, the feeling of his cock deep inside her, left her yearning for more.

But she'd said just that night.

He had been gone in the morning when she'd awakened. No goodbye. No thanks for a good time. Not even a note. Just his scent on her sheets and pillowcases was the only thing that proved the night hadn't been a dream.

"You think you can hold down the fort while I run and go get some coffee?" Cashea asked. It was going to be a long day, and if she was going to make it, she was going to need lots of caffeine.

"Of course. There isn't much going on today. Dr. Reddy's schedule is light this week. Mind picking me up something?" Tiff reached into her pocket and grabbed her small-change purse.

"Did I hear someone is going for coffee?" Dr. Cathy Reddy asked, coming out of one of the exam rooms. A warm smile spread across her face. Her gray-streaked brunette hair was tied up in a high bun. She pushed her glasses on top of her head and went toward Tiffany and Cashea.

"I'm going to go down to the coffee shop," Cashea said. She needed to get out and stretch her legs. After hearing how much it was going to cost her, she was going to need to come up with a plan of how she'd pay off the bills. Walking and fresh air would help clear her head.

"If you don't mind grabbing me the largest black coffee they have, I will pay for everyone's." Dr. Reddy chuckled.

"You got a deal." Cashea laughed. A few minutes later, she was stepping outside the building. She slid her sunglasses on and began the brief stroll to the coffee shop that was located a few doors down. The staff from the office usually ordered from this shop. Their coffee was good and their snacks tasty.

Cashea took her time and inhaled the fresh morning air. She wondered if she could get a temporary side job. Something she could work one or two days a week for a brief moment so that she could erase this debt. She hated having anything over her. She may not be living a lavish life, but at least she was able to afford the necessities in life. Maybe she'd get a second job to cushion her savings account a little more, then quit.

But what could she do for a month or two to earn extra money in a small town like Ironhaven?

Cashea arrived at the coffee shop a little too quickly for her liking, but she knew she couldn't take forever. She went in and ordered their coffees. This morning it was only the three of them in the office. The others would be in later in the morning. After placing their orders, Cashea found a spot to wait near the front windows. The shop was busy, and it looked as if it would take them a while to get to her order. She didn't mind waiting. A board on the wall caught her eye. She moved over to it and saw it was filled with job postings, missing animals, properties for rent. One particular flyer grabbed her attention.

Temporary assistance needed.

She moved in closer and read the small blurb.

The Hen House was looking for a temporary wait-ress for weeknights.

"Ask and you shall receive," Cashea murmured.

That would be perfect. She'd run over there tonight after work and inquire about the job. If they only needed temporary help then that would work out for her. She didn't need two full-time jobs. This would help her pay off this credit card and put a bit more money aside for a rainy day. Hopefully, it wouldn't be raining for a long time.

"Well, Tess will be going on maternity leave soon, and we just need someone to cover her while she's out," Clay said. He was the owner of the Hen House.

Cashea had been lucky that he just so happened to be in the bar when she'd arrived. He had been too pleased that she had come to chat about the job posting.

She'd made the walk over after she'd left the office. It had taken her about twenty minutes to make the trip. She hadn't had a chance to give Hal a call yet to tell him to go ahead and fix her car. It had gotten busy with a few same-day appointments that had got added on. By the time she'd looked up, it was too late to give him a call. One thing about small towns, certain places held strange hours. Hal's shop closed at four in the afternoon. She'd just have to call him in the morning. It shouldn't be a problem.

"How long is she expected to be out?" Cashea asked. She bit her lip and leaned against the counter. The dinner crowd was just starting to arrive. Plenty of folks stopped by the Hen House for supper and a good drink. With football season going on, Cashea was sure the bar would soon be packed with people wanting to catch the game and grab a bite to eat.

Mondays were sure to not be as packed as the weekends. It had been a long while since Cashea had waited tables. She'd done it in high school and college to help pay the bills. It would be like riding a bike. Her old tricks would come back to her.

"She said she only wanted to take about eight weeks. How long are you looking for?"

Eight weeks wouldn't be too long. Cashea was sure she could save up her tips she'd get and have a nice cushion in her savings account. This may certainly work out. She glanced around the place through different eyes. She was used to coming in on Friday and Saturday nights for fun. Working Monday through Wednesday for two months wouldn't be bad. Cashea glanced in the direction of where Draven usually sat. Tonight, some other fella had claimed his seat. A sigh escaped her. She needed to put him out of her mind. Their one night together had been mind-blowing, but that was all they would ever have.

One night.

Cashea cleared her throat and turned her attention back to Clay.

"You're sure it's just weeknights, no weekends?" She wanted to clarify this up front. The Hen House was a very busy bar that had large crowds on the weekends. She would definitely know. The house was always packed when she and the girls performed.

"No weeknights. The others have pitched in and will cover her weekend shifts. I only need the three evenings a week covered until she gets back." Clay grinned at her and pressed his hands together in a steeple, playfully begging.

She barked a laugh and shook her head. Clay was a good man from what she'd heard from Danny. He paid his employees fair, and the bar was one of the most popular ones in town. Even people from neighboring towns came over to have a little fun at the Hen House.

Cashea pondered it for all of a few seconds. This would work out. She would cover for Tess while she was out on maternity leave and then go back to working her one job. Cashea stuck out her hand to him. Clay's grin widened even more. He slid his hand in hers and gave it a tight squeeze.

"When do I start?"

Chapter Eight

"Yo, Sarge, we're striking up a card game tonight. You in?" a deep voice with a Southern drawl asked.

Draven turned to see Trent headed his way. Draven leaned against the corral fence and had been watching a few horses graze. He was done for the day and couldn't bring himself to go home. There was nothing wrong with his house, it was beautiful and built how he wanted it. But the only thing was that it was meant for a family. It wasn't for a single man who lived alone.

Draven didn't know when he'd started feeling lonely. He would have thought he would enjoy the solitude of living alone, but he'd have to admit that night he'd spent with Cashea had him feeling as if he was missing out on something.

A woman to come home to.

Someone to share his life with. A loving partner who would make him feel needed and wanted. He shook his head. His father's wish for him to settle down must be messing with him.

Trent came to stand by him. He'd been on the ranch for about six months. He and Draven were close in age, and both had served for about the same time. Trent had done multiple tours in the Army. He had recently retired and joined Silver Creek. He was an overall good guy. Draven didn't mind him too much. He was a hard worker and had one hell of a way with horses.

"I told you not to call me that," Draven murmured. He was retired. No longer did he need to go by his official title and rank from the Marines. Here he was just Draven Harvey. "I'm retired."

"You were ranked higher than me." Trent chuckled. He rested his forearms on the fence and joined Draven in gazing out at the animals.

"We are equal here." Draven ran a hand along his face. A card game did sound good. He did have fond memories of the games the men and women in his battalion had played. He blew out a deep breath and bit back a smile. Those games were legendary. They may not have had much money to bid with, but everyone got creative on what they would wager with.

Draven had planned to head down to the Hen House. He figured he would switch up the days he would go. If he wanted to avoid Cashea, then he wouldn't be able to go on Friday or Saturday nights any longer. Not that he had to avoid her. He *needed* to avoid her. Everything about her had him wanting things that he didn't deserve.

Like another night between her thighs.

"So you in or not?" Trent asked.

"Next time." Draven shook his head. It was rare for him to go down to the bar on a Tuesday, but what the hell. Two of his favorite teams were playing tonight, so this would be one hell of a game to watch, and it would go good with a big thick burger and a nice glass of bourbon or whatever was on tap.

"Well, we'll save a seat just in case you change your mind." Trent gave him a slap on the back.

Draven stiffened. Trent must have recognized his reaction. His smile disappeared. A lot of the men and women who came to the ranch had issues they were dealing with. Some even sought therapy.

One of the local social workers came out to the ranch once or twice a week to meet with a few of the ranch hands on their lunch. It was part of the ranch's agenda to assist the veterans.

"My bad, man. It's a habit."

"Don't worry about it," Draven said. He pushed off the fence and tipped his head to Trent. His reaction was automatic. It was something he was going to have to deal with. Trent wasn't a threat to him. Maybe over time that reaction would die down. "Next time."

He pulled his brimmed hat down on his brow and headed toward his truck. He had already showered and changed his clothes. There was no way he would go out smelling of God only knows what. He got in his truck and took in Trent walking toward the housing for the hands who preferred to stay on the property. His father had ensured that they would have a place to stay if they wanted to be close to the ranch. He'd built a large house they shared.

Draven started his truck and threw it in gear. He drove down the road and passed the main house. He took in his father, Bee, and Buck sitting on the porch. He tapped on the horn and kept going. He didn't want to stop and explain where he was going. If his father knew he was headed toward the bar in the middle of the week, he was sure Andy would try to talk him out of it.

Once on the main road, he stepped a little harder on the gas. He rolled down the windows and allowed the air to flow through the cab. His phone chose that moment to ring. He glanced down at the screen and took in Ridge's name flashing. Draven tapped on the hands-free button on the steering wheel to answer.

"Yeah," he answered dryly.

"Well, hello to you, you old son of a bitch." Ridge chuckled.

Draven relaxed at the sound of Ridge's voice. His brother was younger than him by four years and was probably the only person he would let get away with talking to him like that. Draven was damn proud of him. Ridge's practice was thriving. He was a brilliant vet and he had a long list of clients. He had brought in another vet who helped him handle the in-office visits so he could go out on ranch and farm calls in the community. Ridge loved what he did, and it showed.

"What the hell do you want?" Draven asked, his voice coming out a little more gruff than he had planned.

Ridge just laughed it off. If anyone knew Draven, it would be Ridge.

"Well, I am being made to call you to invite you for breakfast in the morning. We would love to have your bright personality and sunshine at the table." Ridge chuckled again.

Draven didn't have to think twice about his answer. He had already made up his mind that he was going to make a conscious effort to be around his family more. Maybe that would cure this new loneliness he was feeling.

"I'll be there," Draven replied. He was met with silence. He glanced over at the screen and saw the phone call was still active. Had his answer shocked Ridge into silence? "Are you still there?"

"Yeah. I honestly didn't think you would say you'd come," Ridge said.

"Well, do you want me there or not?" Draven frowned. If he hadn't thought he would commit, then why call and ask?

Because he's called and asked multiple times before and you declined.

Draven blew out a deep breath. He needed to do better. His family didn't deserve the cold shoulder from him. They had been trying for years to get him to open up to them.

"Of course we do. It will be good to have you. Bee said breakfast will be on the table at seven sharp."

Draven nodded. That would be perfect. He'd get his day started then take a break to go enjoy breakfast which he was sure was going to be out of this world. The woman was a goddess in the kitchen. The call ended with Draven promising to not be late.

He pulled into the Hen House parking lot and noticed how different it was than on Fridays. Maybe this would be better. How many people truly went out on a Tuesday night? He found a spot and coasted his truck in. Again, he made sure he was in the back away from where most of the patrons would park. He took pride in his truck. It was the first brand-new truck he'd ever purchased. He killed the engine and got out. He glanced over where Cashea's vehicle had been parked and didn't see it. He just hoped Brett heeded his warning. If he had to go back to him, he wasn't going to be as nice as he was last time. He'd been tame and let Brett off lightly.

Draven made his way to the entrance and opened the door. Country music blared from the speakers. The house DJ was on the stage playing the latest music. This crowd was definitely lighter than the weekend. He walked over to the bar and was able to claim his usual spot. There were familiar faces already seated along the dark-wood counter. He slid into his seat and nodded to some cowboys he recognized.

"What brings you in on a Tuesday?" Danny came out of the back with a tray of clean glasses. He set them on the counter a little ways away from Draven.

"Good food, ice-cold beer, and the game," Draven said.

"Hear, hear," a few of the guys murmured, holding their frosted glasses in the air.

Draven gave a small smile at the camaraderie when it came to the game that was just starting. It was already up on the television screen.

"I know what your usual order is, but I have a new orient. I'm gonna let her come take your order. Be kind. Today's her first day, and we can't afford to lose her." Danny chuckled.

"Not a problem," Draven murmured. He wasn't that much of an ass that he would ruin someone's first day on the job. Everyone had to start somewhere. He leaned back in his chair and zeroed in on the television. With the music blaring in the background, the television on the channel he watched with the closed caption, all he was missing was his food and beer.

"She'll be right out." Danny went back over to the glasses and began placing them where they belonged.

The door swung open, and a familiar figure sauntered out of the back. Draven froze in place, his breath catching in his throat.

Cashea.

She wore a pair of knee-high boots and a black V-neck t-shirt and jeans that looked as if she'd been poured in them. Her hair was pulled into a high ponytail, a few wisps escaping. Draven remembered the sight of her hair spread out underneath her on her pillows. The sounds of her moans and gasps came rushing back to him. His heart rate sped up. He swallowed hard and bit back a curse.

Their eyes met.

Draven knew he was fighting an uphill battle when it came to this woman. Her lips curled up into a sexy smile. She moved toward him. She snagged a notepad off the counter and pulled a pen from her back pocket.

"Hello there." Cashea stood across the bar from him.

He greedily took her in, from the light makeup to the scent of her perfume reaching him. He was mesmerized.

She tilted her head to the side. "What can I get you?"

"Hey," he finally replied. He inhaled sharply and leaned forward. He just wanted to be a little closer to her. Thoughts of food had gone out of the window. Instead of ordering food, he said the first thing that came to mind. "Why are you working here?"

She sighed heavily and rested a hip against the counter.

"Well, long story short, my good looks may get me compliments, but they sure as heck don't pay for tires," she drawled.

Draven's hand clenched into a fist. Brett hadn't paid for her tires. He opened his hand and tried to relax, but anger surged inside him. He would take care of this. She shouldn't have to get a second job because an asshole decided to damage her property. If he had to drag Brett to her and make him pay her, he would do it. There were a few things he had mastered in the military, and one of them was how to get a man to talk. He was very skilled at prying things from men.

Brett was going to regret the day he'd first laid eyes on Cashea.

"Brett hasn't contacted you?"

"No," she snorted. She rolled her eyes and brushed a few strands of hair out of her face. Even in the low light of the bar, her skin still glowed. "And I don't expect him to. Between the tow, the tires, and the other thing Hal said I needed, my credit cards can't take any more. Hence why I'm needing a second job. It's only temporary, though, until Tess comes back from her maternity leave."

Draven had half a mind to leave right then and there to go looking for the fucker. He was sure he could find out where he lived with a phone call.

"How'd you get here tonight?" he asked. He ran his hands along his jeans. All thoughts of food and drinks had disappeared.

She smiled and tilted her head to the side again. "Why, the two feet God blessed me with." She giggled. She leaned against the counter and stared at him.

Draven's heart skipped a beat at the sound of her laughter. Even with the music blaring, he heard her. She was fucking beautiful. How the hell could he avoid her? Had he messed up with her by just leaving without saying a damn word to her? He'd just woken up, dressed, and left. He had been a coward. "I had to work my other job before I came here, so it's not a far walk. I need to get out and get some exercise."

Draven remembered distinctly how curvy she was, and she didn't need to lose a damn pound. He liked his women thick. He was a big man and needed a woman who could handle him.

And Cashea could.

That night hadn't left his mind at all. He had to think of something else at the moment. Memories of sinking inside her kept replaying in his head. His jeans were getting too damn tight.

"So, what can I get you?" she continued on.

He cleared his throat and rattled off his order. She took note of it before pushing back from the counter. She tossed him another smile and grabbed a frosty mug. She went over to the tap and filled it with the cold brew.

She brought it back and set it down in front of him. "Enjoy the game. I'll put your order in."

Draven picked up the glass and took a sip of the beer. The Hen House always had the best beer on tap. He tried to focus on the game, but his concentration was shit. He couldn't stop stealing glances over at Cashea. He watched her work the bar with grace and beauty. If he wasn't mistaken, she must have done this before. She had a way about her. Those smiles of hers were infectious. Draven peered around the bar and saw there were a few others eyeing her as she moved around.

Jealousy reared its head, but he had no right to be jealous. He'd had his one night with her. He took another hefty sip of his drink. He was a fucking fool. He could have at least had the decency to offer to take her out to dinner or something. A woman like her deserved to be spoiled by a good man.

Key word, *good* man. That was something Draven was not. It was like taking a cold splash of water to his face and brought him back to reality. He couldn't be what she needed. He exhaled slowly, thankful he'd come to his senses.

"Here you go, honey." Cashea slid his plate in front of him.

That had been fast. He hadn't even realized he'd been daydreaming so long. He glanced up and saw that the first quarter of the game had just ended. She placed a few extra napkins in front of his plate. He stared down and saw the chef had cooked his burger just the way he liked it. The fries were piping hot from the steam still rising from them.

"You need anything else?" she asked.

You, he wanted to stay, but his mouth remained closed. Her being near him was scrambling his brain. He was acting like a schoolboy with his first crush. But most schoolboys didn't get to have their little slice of heaven between the woman of their dream's legs.

"I'm good," he muttered. He was going to have to be.

She walked over, snagged another frosty glass, and filled it up. She brought it over to him and placed it next to his almost empty one.

He gave her a nod. "Thanks."

"Cashea, baby. I need a refill," a voice called out from farther down the bar.

Draven's head snapped around to see who would dare call her baby. His muscles grew tense. He gaze landed on a figure he recognized. Jacob Pierce, whose family owned a cattle ranch south of Ironhaven. Jacob was a good-looking guy and about the same age as Cashea. He was a stand-up guy, but Draven's only problem with him was the use of the term 'baby' when speaking to Cashea.

"I'm coming, Jacob." Cashea smiled. She tucked her hair behind one of her ears and turned to him again. "Let me know if you need anything else."

And then she was ambling over to Jacob. Draven almost called her back to him. He didn't want to see her walking over to some other man. Even though she was at work and doing her job, Draven didn't like the fact that her attention was on someone else. Jacob was a good man from what Draven knew. Last he'd heard, Jacob was even single. Draven only knew that thanks to the gossip he'd overheard at the feed store the other day. What if Jacob asked Cashea out on a date and she accepted? There was nothing he could do about it. She didn't belong to him.

Her hips swaying was hypnotic. Draven had to drag his eyes from those same hips he had gripped the other night. He blinked and focused on his food. He had to stop thinking about her. He snagged his first beer and finished it off. He was going to have to push her out of his head, and maybe tonight was a night where he may need a little help in doing it.

Chapter Nine

Cashea felt Draven's eyes on her the entire night. After she'd served him his food, he hadn't said another word to her. She kept his beer filled and all she got was a muttered word of gratitude, but that was it.

"You've done this before, haven't you?" Danny asked.

Clay must not have shared with him that she'd had experience as a server. She grinned and leaned her hip against the counter.

"Only in college and high school," she teased.

He shook his head and grabbed the bucket of soapy water from the sink and handed it to her. He tossed a cloth in it for her.

"You could have just told me that when you first got here and I wouldn't have been hovering so much." His eyes crinkled in the corners.

"And rob you of the chance to share all of your little tidbits of wisdom?" she joked. She backed away from him with a laugh. For her first night, she'd actually had fun. The tips were good, and by the looks of what she'd made already, she would reach her goal in no time. Maybe after Tess got back she'd ask if she could come in once in a while to help out. She was sure they would still need the staff.

Cashea went over to where a few vacant seats were at the bar. She tried her best to ignore Draven. He seemed to be doing a great job of acting as if she didn't exist. She blew out a deep breath and went to work wiping the counters down for the next person who may want to snag a seat. She moved down to the empty spot next to Draven. She didn't miss the way he tensed slightly as she came close to him.

"Everything all right?" she asked.

He had finished the last beer she'd given him. He'd had plenty, and she wondered if he would be good to drive home. He'd been there for hours, not saying much to the people around him. Just focused on the game and the beer.

"Yeah," he grunted. His gaze remained on the television.

Cashea honestly didn't know how to feel. Their night together must not have meant much to him. Here she was, racking her brains on what she could say to him, and he'd barely glanced her way. Which was saying a lot since she usually wasn't rendered speechless by many. Her nerves were getting the best of her. Should she bring up the other night? Hell, offer him another one? She would be down. His blue-eyed gaze landed on her, and the fluttering in her stomach increased.

Lord, was she in trouble.

"Want another one?" She jerked her chin toward his empty glass.

"I better not." He shook his head.

Her breath caught in her throat as his gaze slid down her. She clamped her legs together while he took in his fill. What the hell was this man thinking? His face was devoid of any expression at the moment.

His eyes locked back with hers. "How are you getting home?"

She blinked, not expecting him to ask that question. She had planned to try to catch an Uber or Lyft. It shouldn't be as bad on a weekday as it was on the weekend. If not, Sara had offered to come and get her.

"Um, I was going to see about an Uber or something," she said. She finished wiping off the counter and dropped the cloth into the bucket. Tonight was her night to be behind the counter. According to Danny, tomorrow he'd have her hitting the tables and walking around serving. She didn't mind doing either. Her skills had been a little rusty, but it was like riding a bike. After the first two customers, everything had started coming back to her.

Draven stared at her for a moment before speaking.

"When do you get off?" he asked.

She glanced down at her watch. Her eyes widened slightly. She hadn't realized the hours had flown by. It was almost time for her to go home. The bar had been busy for a weekday. Plenty of people coming through for a bite to eat and a drink. Whatever game had been on had also drawn the crowd. There had been lots of yelling and screaming for the two teams. Cashea and Danny had their hands full meeting the demands of the customers.

"In about twenty minutes."

"I'll take you home." It wasn't a question but a statement.

Cashea nodded. Something in his eyes hinted that she shouldn't argue with him.

"Thanks," she said. She wasn't going to read much into his offer. He may be a gruff guy who didn't say much, but he was a softy. He didn't have to ask her about her ride situation. Hell, he didn't even have to get involved with the Brett situation but he had. "Want to settle your bill now?"

He jerked his head in a nod and turned his attention back to the television. Another game was on. The last game had finally gone off, and from the sound of the cheers, the right team won. Cashea moved over to the sink and dumped the water out. She rinsed out the bucket and cloth then put them away. She wiped her hands off and went over to the register to get Draven's receipt.

"Need any help?" Danny asked. He came to stand by her and reached for a bottle of whiskey on the glass shelf near her.

"Draven's ready to cash out," she said. She wanted to try to do it herself first. She hit a few buttons on the screen and successfully accomplished what she needed to do.

"Look at you. Fast learner. It took me about a week to get used to this dang computer. Almost threw it out the window, but Clay wouldn't let me."

Danny chuckled. He patted her on the shoulder before heading to a customer.

She took the receipt over to Draven and slid it to him. He pulled his wallet from his jeans pocket and took out a few bills and handed them to her.

"Draven, that's too much," she sputtered. She glanced back down at his receipt, thinking she had given him the wrong one, but it was the correct one. He'd given her an extra two hundred dollars.

"Keep the change."

"I can't accept this." She shook her head and slid the crisp hundred-dollar bills back to him. She didn't need his pity or him feeling bad for her. She was a big girl and she would take care of herself. She'd been doing it for a long time and she would be all right.

"You can and you will."

The deep timber of his voice sent chills down her spine. His large callused hand covered hers and pushed the money back to her. She inhaled sharply at the feeling of his skin on hers. She almost whimpered, remembering how it had felt to have his palms running along her naked skin. Their eyes met, and Cashea was thrust back to that night. She bit her lip, trying to shove away all thoughts of him braced over her. Those eyes had definitely capti-vated her back then, just as they were today.

"The customer determines the tip. Now take it and keep whatever change there is with it."

Cashea hesitated one last time. He squeezed her slightly before releasing her. He slid his wallet back into his back jeans pocket. He reached for his hat that had been sitting in the other vacant seat by him. He plopped it on his head and tilted it back slightly. She slowly slid the money across the counter and went over to finish his transaction. She slipped the tip inside her apron with the rest of her money.

"I shouldn't be long," she announced, spinning around at the sound of a patron trying to get her attention. The last part of her shift flew by. Before she knew it, it was time for her to go. The bar had died down, and besides Draven, there were only a few customers lingering. She walked over to Danny with a small smile on her lips. "So, how did I do?"

He barked a laugh and slapped his leg. "Girl, it was like you've been working here for years. You will blend right on in."

She beamed at the compliment. The Hen House was a great place to come. That's why she loved performing there as well. She glanced around and didn't even see many people throughout the place. A few of the servers were slowly cleaning off tables and getting the place ready for closing.

"You sure you'll be okay if I go now?" she asked. She wasn't sure why, but suddenly she was dragging her feet. Her gaze drifted over to Draven who was still engrossed in the television.

"Of course. How are you getting home? I saw you walked here. It's too late for a pretty girl like you to be walking out there in those streets." A worried expression came over his face. Danny always looked out for everyone at the Hen House. It didn't matter if it was performers who came in to the bar or employees. He always ensured everyone was felt safe.

"Um, Draven is going to take me," she said.

He peered down at Draven and narrowed his eyes on him. He gave a small shake of his head.

"I'm not sure he should be driving," he muttered. He pushed off where he was leaning against the counter and strolled over to Draven. He stood in front of him where he blocked the television.

Cashea followed behind him. Had she missed something? He appeared to be all right to her.

"You sure you're up for getting behind the wheel?" Danny asked him.

"What are you talking about, Danny?" Draven sat back and folded his arms. He pulled down his hat.

"You know I can't let you onto the road if you are inebriated." Danny rested his hands on the counter.

"I'm fine. There is nothing to worry about." Draven eased back from the bar and stood to his full height.

Cashea bit her lip as she watched him sway slightly. Fuck. He couldn't drive. He sniffed and righted himself. He lifted his hat and ran his fingers through his hair, replacing it back on his head. Danny wasn't buying his act.

"Nope. Give me your keys. I'll call Ridge and tell him to—"

"What if I drive him home?" Cashea blurted out. She blinked, unsure where the idea had come from. She jogged around the counter and came to stand beside Draven. She inhaled sharply at the reminder of how much bigger he was than her. She tilted her head back and met his gaze. "I mean, if you are okay with that. Or do you want him to call Ridge?" She didn't know who the hell

Ridge was, but maybe he would prefer him over her driving.

"I'm okay with that as long as he ain't behind the wheel," Danny said.

He and Draven fell into a staring contest, but soon it was Draven who broke.

"She can drive," Draven growled. He reached into his jeans pocket and took out his keys. He passed them to Cashea. She took them from him and held them up so that Danny could see.

"Let me get my bag and clock out." She spun on her heel and hightailed it to the break room, not wanting Draven to change his mind. She flew into the room and went over to her locker. She opened it and pulled out her bag. It was heavy from her work clothes, shoes, and purse she had stuffed in it. She hefted the strap over her shoulder and slammed the door shut. She paused and blew out a deep breath. This didn't mean anything. Her driving him home was helping him out. Maybe she could leave his truck there and then find a way home.

Cashea went over to the time clock by the door and punched out. She left the break room and headed back to the bar. Her heart raced as she walked back through the bar. She didn't see him by the bar any longer. Had he not heeded Danny's warning and left without her? Then she remembered she had his keys. He was near the front door speaking with Tim.

"I'm ready if you are," she announced, arriving at his side.

"You got your car back?" Tim asked.

Cashea shook her head. She had hoped to have her truck back, but according to Hal, she needed something that rotated behind the wheels, and it would be a couple of days before he'd have the ones in he needed.

"I wish," she muttered with a deep sigh.

"She's driving my truck. Danny apparently thinks I'm not good enough to drive." Draven shook his head. A scowl was embedded on his face. He obviously wasn't happy with the situation.

Maybe she should have just let Danny call whoever Ridge was.

Draven moved over to the door and pushed it open. "Let's go."

"See you tomorrow." Cashea tossed Tim a small smile before she ducked out the door with Draven following behind her.

* * *

Cashea kept her hands on the ten and the two. She was a little nervous driving Draven's truck. He hadn't said much but to give her directions to his place. Her heart was pounding. She had never driven a truck this size. Her small SUV was perfect for her. Draven's pickup was an oversized cab and was massive. She would normally make a joke about a person driving a truck this size, but it fit Draven. He needed something this size.

They rode in silence while soft music played from the radio. He may not speak much, but she'd be damned if she would ride in a car in complete silence. Only weird people did that.

Or serial killers.

Or someone plotting someone else's demise.

Cashea bit back a chuckle. This is why she couldn't ride with no music or conversation. There was no telling where her thoughts would go.

She glanced over at him, but she couldn't see his eyes. He had his hat pulled down low. She didn't even know how he was able to give her directions without paying attention to the road. She had already decided that once she got him safely home, she would call someone. If Sara didn't answer, she was sure Monica wouldn't mind coming to get her.

"Who's Ridge?" she asked to break the silence.

She wasn't even sure if he was awake. His chest rose and fell in a slow rhythm. For a moment he didn't respond. Her hands tightened on the steering wheel. Maybe he was sleep. Or maybe he was sitting there regretting that she was driving him home.

"My brother."

Cashea jumped at the sound of his voice. She glanced over and watched him take his hat off. He tossed it in the backseat then ran his fingers through his hair. She turned back to the road before she did something drastic like pull over and hop into his lap.

"Who's older? Do you have other siblings?" She winced. *Way to go, girl. Now he's definitely going to think you are the weirdo.*

But she wanted to know more about him. Was that so wrong? Hell, she had already slept with the guy. She knew his name, he was retired military and he was a cowboy. It wouldn't kill her to at least know a little something about him.

"I'm the eldest, and it's just us two."

And they were back into the silence. He really was a man of few words. The turn Draven had mentioned was coming up. She slowed the truck down and guided it onto the new road. A few minutes later, a sign that spanned over the road welcomed them to the Silver Creek Ranch. They came to a fork in the road.

"Right."

Cashea nodded and followed the road. A few more turns, and they were drawing up to a beautiful home with dark shutters and an oversized wrap-around porch with a swing. It was Cashea's dream home. She loved the farm-style homes. She knew without even going in that the kitchen would be large and fitting for someone who lived in the country. She loved to cook and wished she had someone other than herself to create meals for.

"Wow. Your home is gorgeous." She parked the truck in one of the two spots in front of the house. Even in the darkness she could appreciate his home. There were a few lights left on the porch that allowed her to see some of it. She leaned forward, trying to take it all in.

"Thank you."

Cashea turned and found Draven staring at her. She reached up and tucked her hair behind her ear. She looked down at her hands, unsure of what to say or do.

"I wasn't thinking when—"

"Do you want to come in?" Draven asked.

Cashea flicked her gaze to him. The tension in

the cab was thick. Cashea's heart raced. She should say no and snag her phone to call someone to come and get her.

But instead, she found herself nodding.

"I'd love to."

Chapter Ten

Draven led the way into his home. He wasn't sure what the hell he was doing. All he knew was that he didn't want Cashea to leave. The sound of her gasp when his house came into view had done something to him. He had taken his time when designing the home. He'd tried to think of everything that would be needed in a sprawling country house on a ranch. When his father had approached him to come up with plans for the house, it had been years before he had retired. Why had he built a house this size? He'd like to think he had thought of everything that would be needed and desired in a home, but the one thing he was missing was someone to share it with.

But what he'd learned about himself by the time he had retired from the military was that he would be better off alone. At least that was what he had thought until he had met her. His hands were covered in blood for his country. He had become a monster all in the name of freedom. He was a soldier acting on orders.

Now he was no longer that person.

When Cashea looked at him, she didn't see anything but Draven. He liked the way she took him in when she thought he didn't know she was staring at him.

He swallowed hard as he led her through the house. It amazed him that he had led full battalions into battles and completed missions, but when it came to Cashea, he froze. He didn't know how to be the man she would need. He wasn't even sure what she wanted.

Hell, what did he want?

Peace.

He wanted that little piece of Heaven that he'd experienced with her. Her smile, her laugh, the softness of her skin against his had him feeling things he had never thought he would experience.

"You live here all by yourself?" she asked.

They had already been through part of the

home. He had figured by the way she'd reacted that she'd want a tour.

"Um, yeah. I do," he said.

She followed behind him closely, and they went into the kitchen. He reached over and flipped the light on and didn't miss the small gasp that escaped her. He stepped to the side as she brushed past him. Her big brown eyes were round as saucers. She moved to the center of the kitchen and walked over to the large island. She ambled around it, sliding her hand along the marble counter. Draven paid attention to her and her reactions. It was easy to see that she was impressed.

"Oh my, look at the stove." She rushed over to the six-burner, name-brand stove that had set him back a pretty penny. It was said to be the best on the market. Not that he cooked much. He could do a little something in the kitchen if he needed to. "I've seen one like this on the home network, but I never seen it up close and personal."

She flew around the room, squealing with delight at each discovery. Who the hell would be excited about appliances and pantries in a kitchen? Draven couldn't take his eyes off her. She went over to the double doors that led out to the back porch.

She pressed her nose to the window and tried to look out through the glass.

Draven pushed off the doorjamb and strolled over to the light switch for the back porch. He flipped it so she could see. He watched her expression light up. He wished it was daylight so she could see what he got to see every morning. There was nothing better than sitting out on the porch with a cup of coffee first thing when the sun breached the horizon. It was an amazing sight, and he wished he could share that with her.

His cold heart cracked.

Was he truly wanting more?

"Draven, you have a beautiful home." She turned to him with a soft smile on her lips. She leaned back against the door. Her hand lifted and tucked strands of her dark hair behind her ear.

Draven's gaze coasted from her big brown eyes, to her plump lips, to the swell of her breasts down to her wide hips. He stood before her, trapping her between him and the glass.

He reached up and cupped her face. She leaned into his palm, her eyes not wavering from his. Those plump lips of hers curved into a soft smile.

"Maybe one more night?" she whispered.

"Yeah." Draven swooped down and captured

her lips with his. He couldn't help himself. He was supposed to stay away from her, but she was wearing down on the walls he had erected around himself. Her sigh, the feeling of her large mounds crushed between them, and those small fingers of hers entwining themselves in the hair at the base of is neck had him in a desperate need to sink inside her.

He wanted Cashea, but he didn't know how to tell her that.

He may not be a man who was good with words at the moment, but he would show her.

He broke the kiss and took his time blazing a trail of hot kisses along her jawline and down to her neck. He nuzzled the column of her throat and inhaled. Her perfume was intoxicating. He didn't know what it was, but it would always remind him of her. His tongue slid along her skin, taking a taste of her.

Cashea's fingers tightened in his hair. He welcomed the pain. Between that and the pleasure he was sure to find between her legs, it would prove that he was alive.

He reached for her shirt and tugged it over her head. His gaze greedily took her in. She had on a pale-pink lace bra that did nothing to hide her large dark areolas. Cashea didn't hesitate to do the same to his shirt. They both found their way onto the floor. She traced the lines of his chest with her fingertips. She moved down to his abdomen until her fingers came to rest on his belt buckle.

"Cashea," he murmured.

"Don't speak." Her finger came to rest on his lips. Her wide eyes met his as she shook her head.

His heart raced, and he fell victim to the depths of her brown pools. Everything about this woman captivated him. He couldn't—no, wouldn't—resist any longer.

"Just me and you. No thinking. Just enjoying each other."

She reached up and brought his head down to hers. Their lips met in another hot, passionate kiss. Draven tilted his head to the side and reached for her. His hand settled on the base of her neck to hold her to him. In the morning, he'd tell her how he felt. That he wanted to explore what this was between them. He didn't want her thinking he was only using her for pleasure.

He needed more.

The pile of clothing on the floor grew until they were both completely naked. Cashea's body was made to be worshiped, and he was going to do exactly that. Just not in the kitchen up against a glass door. He bent down and swung her up in his arms. She giggled and wrapped her arms around his neck, and he stalked out of the kitchen.

"What's so funny?" he asked. He arrived at the stairs that led to the second floor. He hadn't taken her up there during the tour. She could see the rest of the house in the morning.

"I'm too heavy. I've never had anyone just pick me up and carry me the way you keep doing." Her warm breath skated along his neck.

He took the stairs in an easy jog. He didn't even want to think of the men who she had been with before. She didn't weigh that much. He'd picked up bales of hay that weighed more. Hell, the equipment he'd had to adorn when he was deployed weighed more. What type of men—

No, he wasn't going to go there.

He arrived at his bedroom door and nudged it open with his foot. He hadn't left any lights on when he'd gone out earlier. He really didn't need to. He knew the layout of his room like the back of his hand. He gently placed Cashea down onto the bed. He reached for the lamp on the nightstand. He needed to see her. He flicked the light on and turned back to her. His breath was snatched from his lungs.

She was perfect.

He had never imagined any woman in his bed. He'd never brought anyone here before. She was the first woman to grace the four walls of his private domain.

Her brown skin practically glowed in the low light. He inhaled sharply and had to rein in the animalistic urges he had. Cashea deserved to feel like the beautiful woman she was. He had seen the insecurities in her eyes their first night together. He wanted to erase all the doubts that may linger in her brain. There was nothing wrong with her.

He took hold of her ankle. It was so tiny and delicate in his hand. He caressed her skin, sliding his hand up her calf. She propped herself up on her elbows and watched him. Her legs fell open, revealing her core. His already hard cock swelled even more. He ignored it. This was about her. He crawled onto the bed and braced himself over her. She fell back onto the mattress. He followed her down and took her lips in a crushing kiss.

Here with her, he didn't have any worries or cares. Those demons that haunted him were silent. He focused on the woman who made him feel. His tongue swept inside her mouth. She met him unabashedly. Her arms came around him and locked him into her. Her moans and sighs drove him crazy. He needed to hear her scream. Wanted to feel her body shake as it had before.

He broke the kiss and moved down to her tantalizing breasts. They were worthy of his attention. They filled his hands perfectly. He suckled and licked both of them. He wasn't going to rush this night. He cupped one of the mounds and brought it to his mouth where he drew the nipple deep into his mouth. Cashea's back arched off the bed. Her hips gyrated against his stomach.

"Draven," she moaned.

He loved hearing his name fall from her tongue. He switched to the other side and repeated the motions. He could lie here all night and day and never tire of tasting her body. He finally went down farther. He took his time kissing and licking every aspect of her that he could. He wanted to memorize every part of her until he knew her body as well as he knew his own.

He arrived at her center. The womanly aroma greeted him. He spread her legs wide and bit back a growl at the evidence of her desire coating her labia.

He slid a finger through her folds, and it came away coated with her creaminess.

"Fuck," he growled.

He dropped his head and ran his tongue through the same path. Her essence exploded on his taste buds. He officially couldn't get enough of her. Cashea's fingers found their way to his hair and threaded themselves through the thick locks. He dragged his tongue up to her clit where he suckled it into his mouth.

Cashea's cry broke the silence. Her grip on his hair tightened, and he feasted upon her. There was no other place he'd rather be than right there. Her thighs shook as he took his time. He'd build her pleasure until she could do nothing but scream through her orgasm. He played with her clit, teased it, tugged on it. Cashea writhed on the bed underneath him, chanting his name.

He pushed a finger inside her soaked core. He was greeted with her tight walls and the slickness that was working its way from her channel. He growled, knowing that when he sank in deep, it would be heaven. He introduced another finger, needing to stretch her out a bit. He was a big guy and didn't want to cause her any pain.

"Oh!" Cashea cried out.

Her hips set a rhythm with his fingers, and he thrust them deep into her. He latched on to her clit and refused to let up on it until she came. Her cries soon turned to shouts. Her muscles grew taut, and the mattress shook from her body trembling. She was close. He could feel it. He rotated his fingers and found the spot he had been looking for. Cashea screamed, her thighs clamping down tight on his head. He pushed them apart while he continued to focus on drawing out her orgasm. Her body flopped onto the bed, spent. Her muscles relaxed, and she just lay on the bed, panting with her eyes closed. He withdrew his fingers from her core and used the next few minutes to lick every ounce of cream that had slipped from her.

Draven sat back on his haunches and flipped her over onto her stomach. He used his hand to raise her onto her knees. He ran a hand along his cock and was greeted with a few beads of his sticky liquid. He took in the sight of her ass up in the air. He ran his hands over the globes before he lined up the blunt tip of his cock with her drenched opening.

He pushed forward and sank completely inside her. Their simultaneous groans filled the air. Her warm channel welcomed him without restraint. Her walls closed around him tight. This slickness from her orgasm allowed him to slip right in. He closed his eyes and gripped her hips, unable to move for a second. Her pussy was made for him. So tight and wet. He was trying to not blow his fucking load right there. Nothing could compare to what he was experiencing at the moment. It was as if he was finally home.

"Cashea." Her name fell from his lips.

She went to brace herself on her hands, but he placed one of his on the center of her back and pushed her down. He didn't want her any other way but how she was. He withdrew slightly and sank in. A moan was ripped from him. Slow and steady was not going to work at the moment. He thrust hard, drawing out cries and gasps from Cashea.

He couldn't stop himself. His hips moved on autopilot; he thrust continuously. It was as if he was possessed. He pounded into her, unable to get deep enough. She took everything he gave. Her hands gripped the bedding. She threw her hips back toward him. The sounds of their lovemaking filled the air.

Draven couldn't catch his breath. Sweat slid down his temple, and his body trembled from his own orgasm chasing him. His balls drew up close, and he could no longer hold back. He bent down over Cashea, covering her back with his chest. Her cries were muffled by the bed, but he felt the way her muscles clamped down on him as she came again. His hips continued their motion, and finally, he tipped over the edge into ecstasy.

He roared, his climax slamming into him. Hot spurts of his release shot out of him and flew into Cashea's womb. His hips slowed, and he thrust again, another wave of his release escaping him. He dragged in air to his lungs and caught himself before he fell completely on Cashea. He paused, leaving his semisoft cock still nestled inside her. Cashea's skin was slick with a thin sheen of sweat. Her head was buried in the blanket. He dropped a soft kiss on her shoulder and bit back a wince.

Fuck.

He hoped he hadn't been too rough with her.

"I didn't hurt you, did I?" A slight panic filled him. He withdrew from her warm sheath and felt the evidence of their activities coat his cock. He rolled to the side of her, trying to catch his breath.

"Hmm?" Her head popped up suddenly.

Her dark hair fell like a curtain over her face where he couldn't see her. She pushed it out of the way, and her gaze fell on him. His heart was already racing, but in that moment, seeing her expression of satisfaction, it skipped a beat.

"Not hardly," she said.

He jerked his head into a nod. He reached for her and rearranged them on the bed where he fell back onto the pillows with her cuddled up into his arms. He pulled the blankets over them and for the first time felt at peace in his own home. He glanced down at Cashea who had fallen fast asleep.

He leaned over and turned off the light. In the morning, they'd have a conversation. He liked her just where she was and hoped she wanted to stay there.

Chapter Eleven

Cashea snuggled down even farther into her cozy cocoon and never wanted to leave. She inhaled and breathed in the warm musk of the figure next to her. A bit of panic filled her. The night came crashing back to her. She opened her eyes and saw a tan chest underneath her face. She blinked a few times and lifted her gaze. Her heart about pounded its way out of her chest.

Draven.

She'd done it again. Slept with the man who she had originally assured him they'd have one night. Not that they had done much sleeping. Cashea remembered dozing off only to soon be awakened by a figure braced over her and her nipple being suckled on. A smile came to her lips at the memory of him sliding back inside her and the tender way he'd made love to her.

Made love?

She swallowed hard. Maybe not made love. Fuck? The first time he'd taken her that night, there was no question that he was fucking her. She hadn't even minded. She couldn't ever remember having an orgasm from only penetration before. The way his cock had pounded in her, the position had been perfect for her clit to be stimulated with each of his thrusts. She shivered from the memory.

She wasn't sure what this was between them, but she had gone and put her foot in her mouth last night. He'd said her name, and an expression she couldn't read had fluttered across his face.

Just me and you. No thinking. Just enjoying each other.

She hadn't wanted to know if he was about to change his mind. She was coming to realize that she had a weakness for quiet, gruff cowboys whose name began with the letter D and ended with the letter N.

Draven looked so peaceful as he slept. His dark hair was tousled from her running her fingers through his soft, thick strands. She couldn't help it. When he'd been between her legs, she had needed something to hold on to while the man sent her to the moon with that tongue of his. There were no scowls or frowns on his face. His chest rose and fell in a slow and steady rhythm.

She should go.

Cashea glanced around and took note the sun was rising. The room was basked in the buttery glow of the sun's rays filtering through the windows. She hadn't got a good look at his room last night when he'd carried her in. She had been too enraptured by the sexy, naked cowboy standing in front of her with his massive cock fully erect. Now that she was able to take it all in, it was beautiful, but definitely the bedroom of a single man. It could do with a woman's touch.

What was she thinking?

Let me get out of here before he wakes up.

She carefully slid to the edge of the bed, and it was then she remembered her clothes were down in the kitchen. She glanced over her shoulder and took in Draven's muscular form. The blanket was dangerously low on his waist. Her eyes lingered where there was a slight bulge underneath it. With a shake of her head, she slowly pushed off the bed, not wanting to wake him. She tiptoed to the door and let herself out. She pulled the door up but didn't want to cause any noise if she shut it completely.

Cashea flew down the hall and the stairs. She found her way to the kitchen, and their clothes were in the exact same spot they had tossed them.

"You little hussy," she muttered, gathering her items. How did she go from driving him home to sleeping with him? The moment Draven had trapped her against the patio door, she'd been a goner.

From the tour he'd given her, she remembered there was a half a bathroom down the hall. She padded that way and went in there with all of her belongings. She quickly used the facilities and threw her clothes on. She tried to fix her hair as best as she could with her fingers. Her bag was still near the front door.

She certainly had the look of someone who had been thoroughly fucked. Her body was already feeling the effects of the bedroom aerobics that had taken place. She opened the door and paused, listening for any sounds that he was awake. She would grab her bag and head out. She'd call Sara and walk toward the main road. Thankfully, she didn't have to be at work at the normal time due to the office having a later start. Today the doctor would be rounding in the hospital a town over and then would come in to see patients.

Not hearing any sounds upstairs, she made a quick dash toward the front door. She scooped up her bag and hefted it up on her shoulder. She paused with her hand on the knob and glanced behind her. She didn't know what she was expecting. Him to come rushing down the stairs to tell her not to go? The man had disappeared before she had awoken the last time with no note or a good-bye. A heavy sigh escaped her. She twisted the handle and opened the door. She stepped down onto the porch and pulled the door up as softly as she could.

"Well, howdy there," a voice shouted.

Cashea froze in place. She released the door-knob and slowly turned around. She blinked, taking in the newcomer who had parked his truck next to Draven's. If she hadn't known she had left her cowboy upstairs sleeping, she would have gone crazy looking at the person ambling up to the house.

And when did he become her cowboy?

The resemblance was uncanny between Draven and this guy. Only this version had a wide grin as he made his way to her. He tipped back his worn Stetson, allowing her to see he had the same eyes as Draven. He was slightly shorter than him and not as bulky.

This had to be Ridge.

"Um, hello," she said. Her heart raced at the thought of being caught leaving Draven's house at the crack of dawn. She would have at least liked to do her walk of shame to the main road alone until she could find someone to come get her. Cashea's cheeks warmed as he took her in. She already knew she looked a hot mess. She automatically reached up and tucked her thick hair behind her ear.

"I'm Ridge." He stopped at the bottom of the stairs and held his hand out to her.

Well, that just confirmed what she was assuming. Not wanting to be rude, she went to him and took his hand in a short shake.

"Cashea," she replied with a small smile. She hoped she appeared calm because she was having a slight panic attack on the inside. Why couldn't the ground just open up and swallow her whole? Why did she have to volunteer to bring him home? He had been tipsy, and for all she knew she had taken advantage of him. Her eyes widened at the thought. How drunk had he been? Would he even remember that she had been there? Or what they had done last night? "And I was just leaving."

"Oh? I don't see a car here. Is my brother coming to take you, um, home?" He coughed.

She narrowed her eyes on him, sure that he was trying to hold back a laugh.

"I have a friend coming to get me. She's running a little late, so I told her I would just meet her at the main road," Cashea lied. She hated to fib, but she didn't want to make his brother look bad. She could have woken Draven up and asked for a ride, but she was too chicken to see him in the light of day after the night they had shared. She reached inside her bag and dug around to try to find her phone.

"Before you go, want to grab breakfast? I was coming to make sure Draven hadn't forgot. He didn't answer his phone last night, so I figured I'd stop by this morning." Ridge's grin grew wider. He folded his arms in front of his chest. He definitely had figured out why she was leaving his brother's house early in the morning.

"Um, thanks, but I can't, and Draven's still asleep."

There went that cough again. He was having too much fun with this.

She still hadn't located her phone. She pulled her arm out of her bag and figured she would search again once she started walking. "I'd better go."

He moved to the side to allow her to pass. She held her head up high and jogged down the few steps, happy she had made it this far. Now she only had to remember how to get to the main road. Her memory was a little foggy from last night, but she was sure once she started, she would figure it out. The bottom of her stomach gave way at the sound of the front door opening.

"Ah, there's my ugly-ass brother," Ridge announced.

Cashea froze in place with her heart practically in her throat. She couldn't help but turn around and glance at the door. Her mouth instantly went dry at the sight of him stepping out onto the porch. He was shirtless but had at least thrown on a pair of gray sweatpants. His dark hair was pushed back from his face, and those icy-blue eyes were locked in on her.

"Where are you going?" Draven ignored his brother. He walked across the porch and stopped at the top of the stairs. He leaned against the pillar in an attempt to appear casual.

"Home." Her voice ended on a squeak. She had hoped she would have been able to disappear before he had woken up. She reached inside her bag again and searched for her phone. If there were any regrets to having a large bag, it was now. Her fingers finally connected with her phone. She brought it out so she could call Sara or Monica to come and get her.

"Walking?" He arched an eyebrow at her.

Ridge's head swung back and forth between her and Draven as if he were watching a tennis match.

A frown found its way to Draven's face. "Why didn't you wake me?"

She bit her lip to keep from saying what she was going to say. It sounded too personal to say that he'd been sleeping so peacefully. Her gut was screaming that he didn't get much sleep. Even though Ridge was his brother, she just kept it to herself.

"I didn't want to bother you." She couldn't believe those words tumbled from her lips.

A dark expression rolled in on his face. "It wouldn't be a bother." He ran a hand along his face before he flicked his gaze to his brother as if seeing him for the first time. "I'm not late."

"I just wanted to make sure you were alive. You didn't answer my calls last night or this morning. So I figured I'd come over to make sure you weren't going to stand the family up for breakfast." Ridge's smile disappeared.

Cashea had a feeling there was more that would have been said had she not been standing there.

"I said I was coming. That means I'm coming." Draven's infamous scowl returned. He motioned to Cashea. "Let me take her home then I'll be there."

"Don't worry about me. I'll find a way home." She offered a false grin then spun around and begun walking. She didn't want to be any reason there was a rift in the family. It was obvious something was going down between the brothers for Ridge to come and make sure Draven showed up for breakfast with their family. She swiped at her phone and opened her contacts so she could try calling Sara first. She cursed seeing how her hands trembled.

"Cashea, stop!" Draven's voice cut through the air.

She kept going and shook her head.

"I'm fine. I'll find a way home. Go to breakfast," she called out over her shoulder. Her heart slammed against her chest. She was panicking and didn't want to lose her shit in front of Draven or his brother. Why didn't she wake up earlier where she could have avoided them? Now she understood why Draven had dipped out of her place before she had woken up. He had avoided an awkward morning after like this one.

"Cashea!" Draven's voice was closer. A hand clamped around her wrist and spun her around.

"What the—" A scream escaped her as she was lifted and tossed over a strong shoulder.

Her bag fell to the ground. Draven bent down and scooped it up and stalked back toward his house. She scrambled to find a way to hold on to him and not drop her phone. She wrapped her arms around him and held on for dear life.

"What are you doing?"

He ignored her and kept walking. She couldn't see where they were going until his truck's tires come into view. He came to a stop by his vehicle and deposited her onto her feet. She stared up at him in surprise. There was a strange glint in Draven's eyes that she'd never seen before. He appeared flustered and not like the quiet, unreadable Draven she had come to know. He raked his fingers through his hair again and stared down at her.

"I said I will take you home," he growled.

He trapped her against the truck. She didn't know how to react. His nearness was doing something strange to her. Her body was responding to him as it appeared to always do. Her gaze flicked over to Ridge who was staring at Draven in shock. He opened the passenger door and motioned for her to get in.

"Let me throw on shoes and a shirt."

"But Draven—"

"Either you get in yourself or I will put you in there myself," he threatened. He rested his hands on his hips and narrowed his eyes on her.

Cashea's mouth opened then closed. She reached for her bag that he had put on the ground and hefted it up onto her shoulder. She lifted her chin and stepped up into the truck. She settled back into the seat while she watched him jog over to the house. She left the door open, figuring she would wait until he came back before she closed it since it was late summer. He spoke with his brother for few moments, then went into the house.

Ridge walked over to his truck that was parked next to Draven's. His driver's door was next to her door.

"It was so nice to meet you, Cashea." He faced the house again to stare at it, turning back to her. His smile widened. "I have a feeling we'll be seeing each other again soon."

"Bye." She gave a small wave to him.

He shook his head and got in his truck. His engine roared to life, and he backed up and drove off.

Cashea sat in a stunned silence regarding the way the morning was turning out. She glanced down at her phone that was still in her hands. Looked like she wouldn't need to call anyone at the moment. She placed it in the cup holder on the center console. She didn't have long to wait. Draven reappeared from his house. Cashea shut her door and watched him stroll to the car.

He got inside and turned to her. They stared at each other for a brief moment, then he reached over and brought her to him. He covered her mouth in a kiss that left her breathless. He pulled back, his hand still resting on the nape of her neck. Her eyes remained closed as she tried to regain control of her breathing.

"Good morning." His low voice sent a chill down her spine.

Cashea opened her eyes and stared into his blue ones. She reached up and ran her finger along his rugged jawline that was still covered with a light dusting of hair. The memory of his bristles tickling her inner thighs came to mind.

"Morning," she whispered.

"Cashea, I like you. A lot," he said.

She froze in place. Her fingers had trailed down to his lips. Those lips had touched every facet of her body last night. Her gaze crept back up to his. Draven's hand slipped away from her neck and came to rest on the back of hers. He took it in his and entwined their fingers together. His was so much larger than hers. It engulfed hers completely.

"I want to see you," he said.

"I'm sitting right here." She couldn't help herself. When nervous, she tended to make jokes, and right now it slipped right out of her.

He was dead serious, but his lips curved up in a slight smile. Her heart skipped a beat. Just the half-crooked smile was enough to change his face completely. She had an inkling of what he would look like with a full-blown smile, thanks to getting to meet his brother.

"You know what I mean." He raised their hands and placed a soft kiss on the back of hers.

This was a gentle side of Draven that she was captivated by.

"I'd like that," she breathed. Hell yeah, she wanted to see him again. She could barely contain her excitement because she didn't want to look like a goofball in front of him. But she did have to clarify what he meant. They hadn't started off on the right foot. Both nights they had ended up in the bed together. Did he mean just continue to sleep with her? She frowned. "Wait. Do you mean take me out on a date or just—"

"I want you, Cashea. As in you be my woman."

She blinked. Be his woman? She smiled and gave a nod.

"I want you, too, Draven and I like the sound of that."

Chapter Twelve

They were being followed. Draven glanced in the rearview mirror casually and took note of the two pickup trucks that were about a quarter of a mile behind him. He focused back on the road. Cashea's hand was still clasped in his. He hadn't wanted to let her go since he had taken hold of it.

When he had awakened, he had panicked, thinking she had left. He was surprised that she had been able to get out of bed without him waking up. The last time he had slept so deeply was at her place. There was something about this woman that kept the nightmares away. Being with her soothed his soul, and he refused to lose her, and seeing her trying to walk away from him had set him off.

It was out of character for him, but he needed to have her hear what he had to say. He had figured they would have a chance to talk when they woke up. He'd kept her up pretty late. He hadn't been able to get enough of her. Having her in his bed did something to him. His dick was hard right now thinking of what it felt like to sink deep inside her. Cashea's small sighs, moans, and cries still echoed in his head.

Even though they had only recently met, he already knew she was meant for him. He would take his time and court her. That was what his father would recommend.

Hell, the old man was going to get a kick out of the notion that he had found a woman. Andy and Bee would probably start trying to plan his wedding the moment he brought Cashea to the main house to meet them. Marriage didn't seem like a such a bad idea anymore. He was shocked that the thought had even entered his head. He had been so against it before, but now that he had met Cashea, it was an option he was willing to consider.

Cashea was staring out of the window. She hadn't said much, but he was all right with that.

"I need to stop at the gas station. It won't take me long," he said.

"That's fine." She looked over at him with a small smile.

Her beauty took his breath away. How the hell was he so damn lucky that she would even give him any of her attention? There were certainly better men than him she could be with. He loved seeing her smile at him. He even felt the strange movement of his lips curving in an upwards tilt. He hadn't had much to smile about in the last few years.

Until he'd met her.

They soon arrived near the center of town, and still those two trucks were trailing behind at a safe distance. Draven would make a stand in the gas station parking lot. There was little doubt in his mind that it was a coincidence that the two trucks were going in the same direction as him. He didn't need any weapons to defend himself. He could thank the Marines for all of the skills he'd been taught. He glanced over at Cashea. He didn't care who came for him, no one would ever touch her.

He pulled into the gas station and parked near a pump. There was a single car near the storefront of the station. It was bright and early, and not many people had been out on the road. His tank was a little less than full. He killed the engine and checked on Cashea.

"Want anything?" he asked.

"No, I'm good." She shook her head and gave a little squeeze to his hand.

Unable to resist, he tugged her to him and pressed a hard, quick kiss to her lips. He wanted more, but he had made a promise that he would be at breakfast. Ridge didn't seem too convinced that he was going to make it.

"She's a pretty little something," Ridge said.

His younger brother had a twinkle in his eyes. Cashea leaving his house early in the morning would not be a secret. Draven was sure Ridge would go blabbing to their father and Bee.

"I don't know what I'm doing," Draven admitted.

The last relationship he had been in, she had cheated on him almost every single time he'd been deployed. That was about six years ago when he'd broken up with her. Draven hadn't thought about Brooke in a long while. Because of her, he had decided he wouldn't enter into any relationships while he was still enlisted. By the time he'd retired, he didn't think he was even fit to be around the ranch animals.

"She's obviously here for a reason. Be your grumpy-ass self. I don't know why, but she likes

you." Ridge grinned and slapped him on the shoulder.

Draven studied Ridge and saw nothing but brotherly love in his eyes. Draven relaxed and gave a nod. Ridge was right. She apparently didn't mind his gruff nature.

"I'll be there for breakfast," Draven said.

"Look, I got worried when you weren't picking up the phone. You know it means a lot to him that you come around," Ridge said.

Draven glanced away and stared out into the yard. He knew his father wanted him around them more. He even realized that. His family was all that he had, and they had always been behind him.

"We all want you there."

"I know. As soon as I take her home, I'll be right there. I promise." Draven turned back to him. His word was always good. He never made a promise he didn't keep.

"Good, and when you come back, I've just got to know how you pulled her." Ridge grinned wide.

Draven rolled his eyes at him and walked up the stairs.

"Hell if I know. Maybe my winning personality," he muttered, going into the house.

Ridge's laughter echoed behind him.

Draven blinked and came back to the present. He dropped another kiss on Cashea's lips before exiting the truck. Ridge's question still played in his head. What was it about him that made Cashea drawn to him? He didn't know, but he would thank whatever higher power that was out there that she was. He was one lucky son of a bitch. He slammed the door shut and casually looked around the gas station.

Just as he figured, the two trucks pulled in. Draven's gaze narrowed on the oversized pickup truck. He immediately recognized it now that it was closer.

Brett.

And he wasn't alone.

"Lock the doors," Draven said to Cashea through the window.

Her eyes widened, but she didn't hesitate to obey. He was satisfied to hear the click of the lock engaging. He pushed away from the truck and walked to the back of his vehicle and opened the door to the gas tank. He moved over to the pump to choose his gas.

"Harvey," Brett called out. The slamming of doors cut through the air, followed by chuckling.

Draven stiffened. He glanced over and took in Brett strolling over to him with about four other men. Draven wasn't worried about the odds.

"You don't want to do this," Draven warned. He continued what he was doing. He pulled his wallet out of his back jeans pocket and took out his credit card. He slid it in and followed the prompts on the screen. "So why don't you and your friends go back home before someone gets hurt."

"Oh, really?" Brett snickered.

He and his friends shared a good laugh. Draven didn't find anything funny. He certainly wasn't a comedian so he didn't know what they found so amusing. He put his credit card back in his wallet and popped it back in his pocket. He lifted the nozzle and inserted it into the truck to allow it to start filling up. He angled himself at the edge of his truck so he could take in the friends who Brett had brought with him. They all appeared to be physically fit. He didn't recognize any of them. Draven folded his arms in front of his chest.

"I don't think the person getting hurt is going to be any of us," Brett said.

"I can guarantee it won't be me," Draven growled. He almost felt sorry that they had allowed

Brett to talk them into coming for him. None of them stood a chance against him. "Are you coming to pay for Cashea's tires?"

"Not a fucking chance," Brett spat. He motioned to his friends. "You came to my place of business and decided to try to extort money out of me. Well, fuck you. It's payback time."

"I'm going to warn you one last time. All of you." Draven met each one of their eyes.

Brett was about to land all of these men in the hospital. A deadly calm came over him; it had been a long time since he'd had this feeling. He was a rancher now, no longer a soldier, but old ways died hard. He took a few more steps away from his truck toward Brett and his goons. He had never wanted Cashea to see this side of him. He had wanted to bury the darkness that lived inside him, but apparently it needed to come out one last time.

He relaxed his arms at his sides.

"You can end this right now, Brett. Give her the fucking money to pay for what you did."

"So what, I fucking slashed her damn tires. The bitch needed to learn to appreciate when a man is trying to give her his attention," Brett snarled.

His friends circled Draven. He sensed their positions without looking around.

"I told you, don't call her that," Draven growled. The shit hadn't learned his lesson before. It would seem that Draven would have to teach him again. Only this lesson was going to stick.

"Oh, so you're fucking her." Brett's gaze flicked over to Draven's truck. He barked a laugh. "That bitch doesn't know a good man when she sees one if she's with you."

Draven's rage reared its ugly head. He wouldn't stand for Cashea to be disrespected. He was certain she could hear the entire conversation.

Brett motioned to his friends. "Fuck him up."

Draven relaxed into a defensive stance as they came at him. He wasn't worried that it was five against one. If they knew what he was capable of, they all would have heeded his warning. The first one swung at Draven, but he was able to dodge the hit. Draven was fast and swift with his response. Two maneuvers, and the man was left writhing on the ground.

Draven turned in time to block the next fist. He had trained for years, and none of these men matched him. If Brett wanted to be dirty and have his buddies jump him, then Draven hoped Brett would visit them in the hospital, because that's where they all were headed. Draven didn't give any of the men an opportunity to breathe. His movements were fast and precise.

"Who is this fucker?" One of them grunted.

They all must have assumed they would be able to easily overpower Draven. Everyone in town may have known he was a Marine, but they would never know the dangerous man the military had released into civilian life. Draven's fist landed on his jaw. A reverberating crack echoed behind it. He would be eating through a straw for a few weeks. Hands gripped Draven from behind, but it didn't matter. He was able to break the hold and spun around. The guy's eyes widened; Draven turned on him. A growl escaped Draven. He threw a punch at Draven and narrowly missed. Draven rushed him, landing two of his own punches. It had been a long while since he'd had to physically defend himself, but his motions were automatic. They could even be considered artistic.

Within minutes, all of Brett's friends lay spread out on the ground. Draven was barely out of breath and riding the high of his adrenaline. He hadn't been in control of himself. His basic instincts had taken over. That was something he had learned to hone in the military. Kill or be killed. He turned just in time to see Brett swinging a bat at him.

"Dodge this!" Brett shouted.

Sirens blared in the background, coming closer. Draven ignored them. He raised his arm just as the bat connected with it instead of his head. Draven ignored the pain. He used Brett's momentum against him by grabbing on to the bat himself and yanked Brett to him. His fist hit the side of Brett's face. The bat fell to the ground, forgotten. Draven snatched Brett by the shirt and lifted him and slammed him on the ground.

He followed him down and launched his fist into Brett's face. Satisfaction filled him at the sound of nasal bones cracking. Draven drew his arm back again and repeated the action.

"That's enough. You're going to kill him," a voice snapped.

Arms encircled Draven and pulled him off Brett. Draven growled and tried to throw them off him; they struggled to drag him away from Brett. Draven's gaze was locked on the unmoving form of the ass who had started all of this shit.

"Sheriff's department. Stand down."

Something clicked in Draven's head. The fight went out of him. They quickly flipped them over and yanked his arms behind his back. Cold, hard steel clamped down around his wrists. He lifted his head, and it was then he took in the scene. Brett and his men were laid out on the ground of the gas station. Patrol cars with flashing lights had entered the station and were parked around them.

"Draven!" a familiar voice screamed.

He jerked his head around and saw Cashea being held back by a uniformed officer.

Tears streamed down her face. "Why are you arresting him? They attacked him!"

"Please remain calm, ma'am. We need to finish securing the scene," the officer said.

He pushed her back, and that move didn't sit well with Draven. He growled and tried to get up but he was immediately restrained even further with two knees to his back.

"Stay down," one of the two officers who held him down snarled.

The handcuffs wouldn't truly hold him back. He growled again, needing to get to Cashea. He needed to explain what she had witnessed. Now that he was coming back to himself, he needed her to understand that he was no longer the person the military had groomed him to be.

"Please let me go to him," she hiccupped.

Her eyes connected with his, and the fight went

out of him. She appeared to be safe, and there was no disgust or horror on her face. There was nothing but concern.

For him.

"You are arresting the wrong man. He was defending himself. They jumped him," she cried out.

She tried to get past the officer again, but he held her back.

"Stop touching her," Draven yelled. He bucked again.

The officers holding him down cursed and pressed their entire bodies down on him.

"Ed, let her through," someone shouted.

Cashea dashed past him and sprinted over to Draven. She fell to her knees next to him. He relaxed now that he could see her up close and personal. She didn't have a scratch on her.

"Did they hurt you?" She sniffed.

"Are you okay?" he asked. He ignored her question. The only thing that would have caused him true pain was if something had happened to her. Outside of his knuckles, he was fine. They would be swollen and painful for a while, but they would heal.

"I'm okay. Officers, he was the victim. Why is he in handcuffs?" she asked.

"Ma'am, he's not under arrest yet until we figure out what the hell happened. If you don't mind going with Deputy Jackson and giving your statement, it would be much appreciated."

"But Deputy Robinson, Draven didn't do anything," Cashea snapped. His woman was fierce and determined to argue on his behalf.

"Miss, please. Allow us to do our job." The deputy's voice was filled with frustration.

"I'm fine, Cashea. Take my truck and go home," Draven said. He recognized the stubborn tilt of her chin while she glared at the deputy. He didn't want her to be here any longer than necessary. He just wanted her away from this place and home where she would be safe.

"I'm not leaving you. I'll call your brother," she said.

He jerked his head in a nod. Ridge would notify their father. Draven wasn't worried about being taken down to the police station. Cashea was right. He'd defended himself as he was allowed to do.

Ambulances had arrived, and the EMTs were seeing to Brett and his cronies. Draven bit back a grin at their moans and groans. He was willing to bet they would think twice about coming for him again.

"My phone is in the car," he said. He rattled off his password to her so she would be able to unlock it.

The deputies finally removed their knees from his back and assisted him up to his feet. He stood to his full height and glared at Brett who was sitting on a gurney holding a bloody cloth to his nose. Brett immediately looked away from him. Draven smirked.

He isn't so tough now.

"Come on, Harvey." Deputy Robinson guided him toward a patrol car.

The other deputy walked alongside him. They escorted him to the vehicle then placed him in the back. He grimaced at the small space. His long legs were cramped. Hopefully he wouldn't be back here long. He glanced out of the barred window and took in the chaotic scene. There were plenty of sheriff patrol cars and ambulances. A small crowd was standing off the side of the gas station behind the yellow tape that the police must have put up.

Draven leaned back and blew out a deep breath. His heart was still racing away. He inhaled and focused on gaining control of himself. He closed his eyes, and within minutes his heart slowed down. He was no longer a soldier. He no longer had to fight his way out of situations. He was just a rancher. He didn't start shit.

He just knew how to end it.

Chapter Thirteen

Cashea gripped the steering wheel as she pulled into the parking lot of the sheriff's department. She found a spot to park in and shut the truck off. She settled back in the seat and blew out a deep breath. She couldn't believe what she had witnessed at the gas station. It had been five against one, and Draven had come out the victor.

The moment she'd seen the men get out of the trucks, she had known something was about to go down. She had immediately snagged her phone and called the police. Brett and those men weren't there by chance. Had they been watching her and Draven? Had they followed them? How did they know where they would be? A chill went down her spine at the memory of the men converging on Draven.

She had never seen anyone move like he had. It was like watching a movie. He had been incredible. But his expression had scared her. Mentally, he had gone somewhere else. All Cashea could do was scream at the operator to send the police immediately. The second she'd seen the patrol cars pull up, she'd jumped out of the truck. She had needed to get to him to make sure he was safe.

His feral eyes had swept in her direction as if to make sure she was fine. He was the one who had been jumped, and he was looking for her.

She grabbed Draven's phone and typed in the password. She found his contacts and was able to locate Ridge's number. Her heart was still racing. She just hoped Draven would be okay. The deputy said he wasn't under arrest. So why had they handcuffed him and taken him away?

She hit the number, and Ridge's voice came on the line almost immediately.

"Don't tell me you aren't coming." He sighed.

"Um, hello. Ridge?" Her voice shook as she tried to get control of her emotions. She reached up and wiped the wetness that suddenly appeared on her cheeks. She blinked back tears that blurred her vision.

"Cashea?"

"Yeah, it's me." She cleared her throat.

An officer came out of the building and strolled over to his patrol car. She turned her attention back to the phone. She placed it on speakerphone.

"Where's my brother? Is everything okay?"

"I don't know—"

"What do you mean you don't know? Where is Draven?" he asked.

A door slammed shut in the background. Cashea sniffled and straightened in the seat.

"We stopped for gas before he took me home. These guys came and attacked Draven. I've never seen anything like it."

"What do you mean they attacked Draven?"

"They jumped him or at least tried to. He's been taken to the sheriff's department. I haven't gone in there yet. I told him I was going to call you."

"You did good in calling me. Were you harmed?" he asked. The tone in his voice suddenly changed. A deep murmur of male voices could be heard in the background.

"No, he made me stay in the truck."

"He didn't, um..." He hesitated for a moment.

Cashea closed her eyes, already knowing what he wanted to ask. With the way Draven had moved while fighting those men, she was sure he could have really injured someone. But Brett and those men had it coming. How dare they come and jump him. For what reason?

"No, he didn't. They all were banged up pretty good. I think he broke one of their arms, though. Brett's nose looked to be broken. But they all were alive, at least when I left." Her words were met with a heavy sigh.

Ridge's voice became muffled as he was speaking to someone else before he came back to her.

"We're on our way. Just sit tight, Cashea. My brother, I'm sure is fine."

She nodded, forgetting that he wouldn't be able to see her. Ridge disconnected the call. She took off her seat belt and reached for her bag. She couldn't sit out in the parking lot. She had to find out if he was okay and if they were going to release him if he was not under arrest. She grabbed his keys and phone and exited the truck.

Cashea held on to the strap of her bag and entered the building. A receptionist sat at the counter typing behind a glass window. The waiting room was small with only a few chairs and a window that faced the parking lot. An old coffee pot sat on a small table in the corner. The scent of freshly brewed coffee greeted her.

"Can I help you?" the woman asked. Her face was tan and full of laugh lines around her eyes and the corners of her mouth. Her dark-blonde hair was streaked with gray and was pulled up into a bun on top of her head. She looked at Cashea over a pair of tiny reading glasses as she approached the desk.

"Hi. They brought in Draven Harvey," Cashea announced. She tightened her grip on her bag to try to control the trembling. She didn't know what to expect but she hoped she would be able to see him soon.

"Yes, he's getting processed."

"Processed? But Deputy Robinson said he wasn't under arrest," she exclaimed. What was going on? She leaned against the counter and took in the woman's name on her ID badge. Officer Gamble. "Can I see him? At least let him know that I'm here?"

"No visitors," Officer Gamble said. She pointed over Cashea's shoulder. "You can have a seat, and when they are done, I will let Deputy Robinson know you are here."

"Are they arresting him?" she asked.

"Miss—"

"Moss. My name is Cashea Moss, and I was with Draven. Please, Officer Gamble. Is there anything you can tell me?" Cashea asked. She bit her lip and hoped the woman could tell her just a little something. It was tearing her apart not knowing what was going on.

Officer Gamble removed her glasses and set them down. "Look, Miss Moss. There is nothing for me to share with you at the moment. As I said, they are processing him. That's all I know. Now if you have a seat, I will let the deputies know you are here."

Cashea sniffed and turned around. She walked over to the corner where a few chairs were positioned together. She didn't know how long it would take for Ridge to get there or who else he was bringing. She placed her bag on her lap and wrapped her arms around it. She didn't care how long she had to stay there, she wasn't leaving without seeing Draven.

Remembering that she was supposed to go to work, she pulled out her phone and sent a quick text to the office group chat that an emergency had come up and she wouldn't be in. She hated to call off, but there was no way she was leaving to go to work while Draven was possibly getting arrested. Had they given him medical attention? Why were Brett and his goons allowed to be taken to the hospital?

The waiting room's chairs weren't comfortable, but it didn't matter. She would have to make do. She wasn't going anywhere.

"You don't know why five men would target you and want to do harm to you?" Deputy Robinson asked.

Draven sat back in his chair, thankful they had finally removed the handcuffs from his wrists. He rubbed the skin where the slight imprints had been left.

It was getting harder to bury the anger and rage that was simmering inside him. Brett would certainly pay for what had happened at the gas station. A broken nose was a small price to pay for what he was starting.

"No." Draven flicked his gaze up and met the deputy's. He glanced around the room and bit back a chuckle. He wasn't fooled by the mirror hanging on the wall. Someone was on the other side, watching their interaction. He turned back to the deputy. "Am I under arrest?"

"How did you do it? Five guys coming at you, and you're the only one walking away with a few scrapes and bruises." Robinson jerked his chin toward Draven's hands.

His knuckles were busted and slightly swollen. Outside of that, he felt fine. He had declined any treatment at the hospital. It would have been a waste of time. He'd had swollen knuckles before, and there was nothing a bag of frozen vegetables couldn't heal. He and Ridge had suffered plenty of similar injuries when they were younger.

Draven shrugged, but he knew the answer. It was his military training that he was unauthorized to speak about. He settled back and waited.

"Where were you going at a little after six in the morning?" Deputy Robinson stared at him.

Draven narrowed his eyes on the deputy. These questions were getting quite old. If he wasn't under arrest, he should be able to leave. If he was under arrest, he had a phone call he needed to make.

"Okay, you aren't going to answer that question. Where were you coming from?"

Draven remained silent. A few minutes went by before Robinson gave a nod.

"Okay, one of the officers spoke with the woman who was with you this morning and took her official statement," Robinson said. He leaned forward and rested his elbows on the table between them. "Aren't you a little bit curious about what she said?"

The only thing Draven needed to know was if Cashea was okay. She wouldn't know why Brett and his cronies had showed up at the gas station. Hell, Draven wasn't even sure how they knew he was on the move. The only thing he figured was that they had been watching his house. He made a mental note to increase security around the ranch. He needed to leave here so he could go and see for himself that she was unharmed. The tears that had streamed down her face had just about torn his heart out.

He just hoped that he hadn't ruined any chances of them actually moving forward with their relationship. It may have only been a short time, but he felt it deep down in his gut that he needed her. It had never steered him wrong in the past, and he wasn't expecting it to now.

"Again, am I under arrest?" That's all Draven wanted to know at this point. If he wasn't, they needed to let him go. He hadn't done anything but defend himself. Hell, he had even held back where he wouldn't have hurt the fuckers too bad.

A chirping sliced through the air. Robinson pulled his phone out of his pocket and read the message. He lifted his gaze and stared at Draven.

"Brett Falco suffered a broken nose and fractured cheekbones. Eric Rudd, dislocated jawbone that is going to require surgery. Ben Walker's suffered a broken humerus and radius that appears to need surgery. Nick Evans suffered a concussion and six fractured ribs, and Gus Cross had almost all of the bones in his right hand broken and his right tibia fractured in three places." Robinson sat back and placed his phone on the table.

Draven kept his face devoid of any emotions. That list proved he had pulled back on what he was truly capable of. They were all lucky they were not breathing through a straw.

Hell, they were lucky enough to still be breathing.

Robinson's phone chirped again. He reached for it and read the new incoming message. Draven kept his gaze on the officer. They were stalling. Trying to see if they could find anything on him, but he already knew what they would find.

Nothing.

"It looks as if the clerk at the gas station has come forward along with providing the video footage of the attack," Robinson announced.

Draven bit back a smirk. He pushed back from the chair and stood.

"I'll see myself out," he announced.

"I'll walk you out." Robinson stood and came around the table. He opened the door and motioned for Draven to exit first.

He moved out into the hallway and followed Robinson through the small facility. Ironhaven's sheriff's department wasn't that large.

"You aren't going to tell me what is going on between you and Falco? I know that you two had an altercation at the Hen House." Robinson was still going to try to squeeze something out of Draven.

"Maybe you should ask Falco," Draven replied dryly.

They arrived near the front of the building. An older woman sat at the counter speaking on the telephone. Robinson rested a hand on Draven's forearm. He tensed and stared down at the man's hand before lifting his eyes. He glared at the deputy. He didn't give a shit who he was, he'd better take his damn hand off him.

Robinson apparently got the message loud and clear. He removed his hand from Draven's arm.

"Well, that's the thing. He's not talking," Robinson muttered. He opened the door that led to the waiting room. He motioned for Draven to go. "We'll be in touch if we have any other questions. You are free to go. Just don't leave town."

"Don't worry. I won't be." Draven stalked through the doorway.

Ridge, Buck, and Andy were standing together near the window of the waiting room, but it was the small figure sitting off in the corner by herself that his gaze latched on to. She appeared tired, but she was still the most beautiful woman he'd ever seen. Their eyes connected, and it was then Draven's heart stuttered.

"Draven!" she exclaimed.

She launched herself from the chair and rushed across the room. He opened his arms just in time for her body to slam against his. He wrapped her up in his embrace. He breathed in her familiar scent and didn't want to let her go. Her arms were tight around his waist while her face was buried against his chest.

"Are you okay? I was so worried about you."

Here he had been, concerned that she would

have second thoughts after seeing him at the gas station. He was a monster and didn't deserve her tears. He reached up and ran a finger along her cheek.

"You don't need to worry about me," he murmured. He relaxed slightly now that he was able to see her up close and personal.

Worry and fear filled her eyes, and he wanted to erase them. Later, he'd ensure she would have other thoughts on her mind.

Someone cleared their throat, snagging Draven's attention. He glanced over and found his father studying him with raised eyebrows. He jerked his head to the door.

"Let's get out of here."

They exited the building and walked toward Draven's truck. Ridge's pickup was parked next to Draven's. He entwined his fingers with Cashea's and brought her close to him. He didn't want her out of his sight. Once they were out of earshot, Ridge turned to him and folded his arms in front of his chest.

"Your brother introduced us to your friend, here," Andy said.

His light-blue eyes, the same as Draven's and Ridge's, had a special twinkle in them. His father was horrible at hiding his feelings when it came to his boys and their love lives. Draven was pretty sure he'd probably already called Bee and told her about Cashea.

"I was going to introduce her to y'all," Draven admitted.

Cashea's head swung toward him. He felt the heat of her gaze on him. He glanced down at her and drew her closer to him. They hadn't had a chance to finish having their conversation. They had a lot to discuss, and eventually he would have brought it up.

"What the fuck happened?" Ridge growled. A scowl crossed his face.

Ridge may be the laid-back one of the two of them, and their bond was tight, but his brother would have been right by his side had he been there. A muscle ticked on the side of Ridge's face. He was pissed off.

"And are we still going to have a problem?" Buck asked.

Draven glanced over at the station before leaning back against his truck. He tugged Cashea next to him, not wanting her to be too far from him.

"Brett Falco. I had a little encounter with him down at the bar," Draven started.

"John's son?" Andy interrupted.

Draven nodded. His father pretty much knew everyone in the damn town. The Falcos had been in the town as long as the Harveys had been.

"Brett was getting handsy with Cashea, and I had to set him straight. The fucker then went and slashed her tires," Draven said.

His brother, father, and Buck all went still. Each of them were military men. His father and Buck were retired Navy while Ridge had served in the Army before he'd come home and gone to veterinarian school.

Draven briefly summarized his visit to Brett at the hardware store.

"Wait, what? Why didn't you tell me?" Cashea exclaimed. She pulled away from him and tilted her head, studying him. She reached up and tucked her dark hair behind her ear. "Is this why he brought his boys to attack you? As payback?"

"They've learned their lesson," Draven said.

Buck appeared to relax slightly. His father's friend was a hard-nosed vet who didn't take any shit from anyone. He was like an uncle to Ridge and Draven.

"Well, until we are for certain, we'll make sure everyone knows to stay alert. They'll be picking the wrong damn ranch to fuck with—excuse my language." Buck's face softened as he looked over at Cashea.

She smiled and leaned into Draven. He liked the feeling of her body resting against his. He could certainly get used to this. He didn't miss the way his father took the two of them in. Draven was sure he and the old man would be having a conversation later about Cashea. He tugged her back to him and held her close.

"I need to take Cashea home so she can go to work," Draven said gruffly.

She shook her head. He raised an eyebrow at her.

"I called off once I got here because I wasn't sure how long they would keep you. I didn't want to leave without making sure you were okay," she said.

Draven softened at her words.

A small smile played on her lips. "If you wouldn't mind taking me home, then I can freshen up a bit."

"You can come to the house, my dear," Andy said. "I'm sure Bee is keeping the food warm for us. You are welcome to join us."

She glanced over at Draven. He would love to have her spend the day with him out on the ranch.

"I'd be happy to join you," she said.

"Well, it's settled then. Let me run her home, then we'll be there," Draven announced. He pushed off the truck and opened the passenger door for her.

She gave a small wave and allowed him to help her up in the truck. He closed the door and turned back to them.

"She's a keeper," Buck said with a grin. He slapped Andy on the back and threw an arm around his shoulders.

"I agree." Andy winked at him while his brother gave him a small salute.

The men who he was the closest to had given their approval of his woman. Not that he needed it, but it felt damn good. Now he just needed her to go meet with Bee.

"Oh, I'm not letting her go anywhere."

Chapter Fourteen

Cashea glanced around at the Hen House and wished she would have listened to Draven. He had suggested that she call and let them know that she wouldn't be able to come in due to an emergency, but seeing how it was only her second day of training, she didn't want to miss it. So she'd gone in, and guess who'd also trailed along with her.

Draven.

She smiled and looked over her shoulder and found him still sitting in his same spot he always claimed when he was there. Only this time, Ridge had accompanied him. It was apparent that Ridge didn't trust Draven to go out alone. After that morning, Cashea actually felt better with Ridge there.

But she didn't know if he was there for the protection of his brother or to protect whoever tried to mess with Draven.

"Do you have any questions?" Asia, one of the servers, asked. She usually worked on the weekends but was helping out since it appeared Tess had to go out on leave a little earlier than expected.

Cashea shook her head. She really didn't have any. Everything was self-explanatory, and with her prior experience, it made serving easier now. When she'd got her first waitressing job, she had been horrible at it. But over time she had gotten better. This time around, she wasn't having any issues. It also helped that it wasn't as busy, and that allowed her to learn the setup and routine of all the servers and the kitchen.

"I'm good. Thanks for letting me tag along with you," Cashea said.

Danny had wanted her to work with the girls on the floor so she could jump in and help where needed. She was fine with it. As long as she stayed busy, that was all that mattered.

"Not a problem. I'm just so happy that they were able to find you so we won't be too short while Tess is out." Asia chuckled. "It's weird seeing you working the tables with us. I'm so used to seeing you up on the stage singing."

Cashea laughed. She and the girls would be getting together tomorrow night to rehearse for this weekend. They had already been exchanging ideas in their group chat on what songs they were wanting to do. She couldn't wait for the weekend. They were going to have so much fun performing.

A couple got up from one of the tables in Cashea's section. She gave a small wave to the woman as she was led toward the exit. It was getting late, and a lot of the customers had started to disperse.

"I'm going to go handle that table real quick." Cashea picked up her tray and headed over to the table. She collected the bills they had left as a tip and slid them into the front of her apron. Tonight's tips weren't bad, and she wasn't going to complain. She piled their dirty dishes on the tray and spun around. She went into the kitchen and placed the dishes where they belonged. She quickly returned out onto the floor so she could wipe the table down and make sure the floor was swept. She always wanted to ensure her section was spotless. She looked around and found Asia tidying up her area.

Cashea's gaze landed on Draven and his

brother. The two had their beers in their hands and were watching the sports news channel where two men were excitedly speaking about the current NFL season and the teams they were predicting to go to the championship this year. She wiped her hands on her apron and ambled over to them. She quietly snuck behind Draven, feeling playful. Ever since this morning, he hadn't wanted to let her go far from him. He had used the excuse of being her ride to and from work, but she was sure he was just being protective of her. It was too soon from this morning, and he was still in protect mode.

She arrived at his back and slowly sent her fingers walking up his spine. He stiffened for a moment before looking over his shoulder. When their eyes connected, he relaxed. He spun his chair around and grabbed her by her wrist and brought her between his legs.

"Hey," he said. His gaze dropped down to her lips.

She automatically sent her tongue out to lick them. His nostrils flared.

"Hi. Having fun?" she asked.

He enclosed his arms around her and held her to him. It would appear that Draven was a very possessive man. He didn't like any of the men looking at her. He glared at any man who stared at her too long. She smiled. It was cute. She could get used to a man who wanted to protect her, treat her like a woman and cherish her.

"I am. I've been trying to get this asshole to come have a drink with me here quite a few times." Draven shoved his brother with his elbow.

"I don't want to hear that bullshit. I've invited you countless times to my place for beers, and you refused." Ridge glanced over at Cashea and tossed her a wink. He was completely relaxed, and she wasn't sure if he was paying attention to all the women who had been staring at him all night. "But now I see why he was always coming down to the Hen House."

"Shut up," Draven murmured.

"Oh?" Cashea raised her eyebrow and stared at Draven. Had he been coming on the weekends because of her? She would be shocked if so. He had never paid her any attention before. "So it wasn't the food, drinks, and football?"

"Don't worry about why I was coming down here. Just know it's nice to have somewhere to get away from the ranch," Draven muttered.

She laughed and patted the poor man on the chest. She wondered if she hadn't come over to him that day, would they even be standing here together?

"Cashea! Go ahead and get out of here. It's dead," Danny called out.

She gave him a thumbs-up. He didn't need to tell her twice.

"I'm going to go get my stuff and clock out," she said.

She leaned up on her tiptoes and delivered a soft kiss to Draven's lips. His arm snuck out and wrapped around her waist and held her firmly to him. His large bulge dug into her stomach. She bit back a whimper at the feeling of him. She pressed another kiss to his lips then pried his arm from around her waist. She quickly made her way through the bar and went into break room.

After she grabbed her bag, she tossed it across her chest and then clocked out. She had spent the day with Draven. When they had returned to the ranch, she'd got to meet Bee who was a beautiful woman who certainly cared for Andy and his boys. The woman had cooked enough to feed a small army. It was a wonder that it all was still warm and fresh by the time they had arrived. After their meal, Draven had taken her out on the stead, and she had loved every minute of it. The land was beautiful and peaceful. No wonder he'd come home to work for his father.

It had been an extremely long day, and she was tired. Tonight, she planned to take a hot shower and then fall into bed.

Draven's bed.

He'd talked her into packing a bag and staying at his place tonight. Not that he'd had to do much to convince her. She made her way through the Hen House and headed over to where Draven and Ridge were seated. Her smile disappeared when a tall, lanky figure cut in front of her and stood in her path. Even in the low light of the bar, the twin black eyes were noticeable. A couple strips of bandages were placed across his nose.

Brett Falco.

"Cashea," he said.

"What do you want?" She stiffened and automatically took a step backward.

He had some nerve showing up here while Draven and his brother were there. Obviously, he hadn't learned his lesson. Her gaze flicked to Draven. As if feeling her eyes on him, he turned around. He stood immediately when he recognized the figure before her.

"Here." He thrust a thick white envelope into

her hands. He shook his head. "I don't want any more trouble. If that is not enough to pay for the damage to your SUV, let me know." He took few steps backward, away from her. He spun on his heel and tore through the bar.

"Was that Brett?" Draven growled.

She nodded. He released a curse and swiveled around. She reached out and grabbed his arm before he could go after him.

"Please don't." She moved closer to him and petted him on the chest. Now was not the time for him to be getting angry. He had a few beers in him, and she didn't want his anger to mix with that. She held up the envelope in her hand. "He came to bring me this."

Draven took it and slid it open. He peeked inside it. His eyebrows rose, and he put the envelope back in her hands. Curious, she opened it slightly so she could look. There had to be a least a few grand in there. Her eyes widened. She quickly closed the envelope and stuffed it down in her bag. There was definitely enough for her to get her car fixed up. Her heart pounded. She was rendered speechless.

So not only did he admit to damaging her car, but he also was going to pay for the damages?

"Come on. Let's go," Draven murmured. His hand moved down to the curve of her back and guided her toward the main door.

She waved goodbye to everyone. Ridge met them at the door before they stepped outside. It was a warm night, and the moon was high.

"I'll see y'all tomorrow." Ridge gave them a short wave and jogged over to his truck.

Draven's large hand engulfed hers while they walked to his car. Once there, he helped her inside and shut the door behind her. He stalked around the hood and got in. She pulled the envelope from her bag and took the money out. She counted it, and her mouth dropped open from the amount that was there.

Four thousand, five hundred dollars.

It would be more than enough to get her car fixed. She stared down at the notes, still in shock that he had come around and given her the money to have her car fixed.

"Thank you." She sniffed. She placed the cash back in the envelope and put it in her bag.

"For what?" Draven asked. He took her hand in his and placed a small kiss to the back of it.

A shiver passed through her. "For standing up for me and for just being you."

She leaned over the console and pulled him to her. She pressed a kiss to his lips and almost melted against him. The kiss was slow, tender, and sweet. Draven's hand cupped her cheek as the kiss deepened. A moan slipped from her. Even though she was tired, she wasn't too tired to keep herself from crawling over the console to sit on his lap now.

But she controlled herself.

At least for now.

She eased back slightly. They were both out of breath. Cashea smiled at him. If he didn't hurry up and get them back to his place, they would have another run-in with the police, and it wouldn't be for fighting.

"Are you taking me home or not?" she asked haughtily.

He stared at her for a moment before he did something she had never seen him do. He smiled. Her heart skipped a beat at the sight.

"Yes, ma'am."

Epilogue

Cashea stood on the stage of the Hen House and smiled. The music blared out around her; the girls went to town on the song they had been playing. She danced around and sang the last run of the hook. Tonight was a little special. It had been almost a year since she had approached Draven. She could not believe how fast time had gone by.

Tonight he sat in his same seat at the bar, but only this time he faced her. Her smile widened as their eyes connected. Her heart swelled with love for that man. He was everything she had ever wanted in a man. Tonight she had a special song she was going to sing in front of everyone to help express her feelings for him. A month ago, she had given up her rental house and moved in with him. It hadn't made sense for them to have two separate residences when she spent most of her time on the ranch with him and his family. She had grown to love the Silver Creek. There was so much to love that she always found something to occupy her time when he was off working.

Everything was going perfectly.

The music changed, and Sara and the girls went right into the next song. The crowd recognized the upbeat track 'Love You a Little Bit' by country singer Tanner Adell. It was one of Cashea's favorites, and tonight, she was going to sing it with a purpose.

She had fallen more than a little in love with this man. She was head over heels in love with him. He had been worried about his flaws and his dark secrets. Some he could share, some he still preferred not to, but that was okay. He was learning to open up. He'd even started taking advantage of the counselors who came out onto the ranch. Cashea was so proud of the strides he'd taken for healing himself.

As much time she had been spending on the ranch and getting to know some of the hands, she could see how much it was needed.

Draven's eyes didn't move from her as she

sang the song. She smiled and danced around to engage the crowd, but really, she was singing this for him. The tipsy women in the crowd helped her sing the hook at the top of their lungs. She bit back a laugh at how horrible they sounded, but no one cared. They were all having fun.

Once the song came to an end, it was time for their break.

"Don't go too far. We'll be back after a short break," Cashea announced. She put the mic in the stand and followed the girls off the stage.

"Hey, I'll meet y'all in the back in a little," Cashea said.

"Sure you will." Sara giggled.

"We know you are going up there to see your man." Monica snorted.

"And?" Cashea grinned. She couldn't help it if she wanted to see him. She hadn't seen him since early that morning before he'd headed off to work.

"I can't wait until I can find a man I can be boo'd up with." Kim sighed.

Lilly placed an arm around her shoulder and led her to the hallway toward the dressing room. "Me and you both, girl."

Sara and Monica followed them down the hall.

Their laughter was drowned out by the DJ blasting a popular song.

Cashea spun around and threaded her way through the crowd. Draven's gaze found her immediately and held hers until she was close enough for him to snag her by the wrist and bring her into him. She went willing into his arms. His strong embrace was where she belonged. She had missed the feeling of him. It had only been since that morning, but it had been way too long.

"Hey," Draven murmured. He lowered his head and immediately took her lips in a hard kiss.

She wrapped her arms around his neck and returned it. She pulled back and smiled.

"Hey there." A sudden shyness came over her. She had just been up on stage singing about how she'd found herself in love with him, and now that she was in his arms, she was all of a sudden shy. Was it too soon to say those three words she'd been dying to say? She didn't think so.

Draven tenderly cupped her cheeks in his large hands. His blue eyes mesmerized her. She leaned into his strong, muscular physique.

"Did you mean it?" he asked.

"Mean what?" She played innocent, even though she knew what he was asking.

His hands slid down her body and landed on her waist. He brushed his lips gently against hers once more.

"That I love you?" she asked.

He gave a nod.

"Yes, I meant it." She reached up and entwined her fingers together at the base of his neck. He was so much taller than her that it was a stretch to do it. She held his gaze and didn't care they were in a crowded bar. "Draven Harvey, I love you."

His lips turned up in the corner, and her heart skipped a beat. She had thought Draven had been sexy before. Smiling Draven was drop-dead gorgeous, and she was the luckiest woman on the planet.

"Cashea Moss, I love you, too," he admitted.

She grinned and leaned up on her toes to offer him her lips. He obliged her and covered her mouth with his. Her arms tightened around him. She never wanted to let him go.

Almost a year ago, she'd taken a chance to just come say hello to the sexy cowboy. Now, here she was, in love with him and in his arms. Somewhere she wanted to be forever.

* * *

Thanks for reading book one of the Silver Creek Ranch! Up next is Owned by the Rancher by Imani Jay! Make sure you snag book two today!

Owned by the Rancher
Silver Creek Ranch 2

When city glam collides with country grit, sparks fly hotter than a branding iron on the range!

Tasha:

I'm Tasha Banks, social media influencer extraordinaire, and I've just landed the deal of a lifetime. The catch? I have to spend a month on a real working ranch. No problem, right? Wrong. The moment I set eyes on Liam Reeves, the ruggedly handsome, frustratingly stubborn rancher, I know I'm in trouble. He's everything I swore to stay away from after my divorce - powerful, attractive, and completely infuriating. But as I struggle to maintain my polished image while mucking stalls and mending fences, I find myself drawn to Liam's raw authenticity. Can I keep things professional when all I want to do is throw caution to the wind and give in to the sizzling tension between us?

Liam:

My ranch is my life. I don't need distractions, especially not in the form of a gorgeous city girl who thinks she can play cowboy for a month. Tasha Banks breezes onto my ranch like a whirlwind in designer boots, and suddenly my carefully ordered world is turned upside down. I tell myself I'm not interested, that she's just a temporary inconvenience. But every time she looks at me with those challenging eyes, every time she proves she's tougher than I gave her credit for, I feel my resolve weakening. As the lines between real ranch life and her social media world blur, I find myself wondering: is one month enough time to risk everything for a chance at love?

Will Tasha and Liam brand each other's hearts, or will their sizzling connection fade like the setting sun over the prairie? Saddle up for a wild ride of passion, pride, and finding love where you least expect it!

Owned by the Rancher is the next book in the Silver Creek Ranch series.
Grab your copy of Owned by the Rancher today!

About the Author

USA TODAY bestselling author, Peyton Banks is the alter ego of a city girl who is a romantic at heart. Her mornings consist of coffee and daydreaming up the next steamy romance book ideas. She loves spinning romantic tales of hot alpha males and the women they love. Make sure you check her out!

Sign up for Peyton's Newsletter to find out the latest releases, giveaways and news! Click HERE to sign up or visit her website www.peytonbanks.com!

Want to know the latest about Peyton Banks? Follow her online:

Also by Peyton Banks

<u>Current Free Short Story</u>

Summer Escape

<u>Silver Creek Ranch (Shared World)</u>

Wrangling Her Cowboy

<u>Lunchtime Chronicles (Peyton's)</u>

Polish Boy

Thick & Beefy

<u>The Keith Brothers</u>

Mr. Hotness

Mr. Arrogant

<u>Blazing Eagle Ranch Series</u>

Back in the Saddle

Knockin' the Boots

Roping a Cowboy

Country at Heart

Cowboy, Take Me Away

Hard to Forget

<u>Special Weapons & Tactics Series</u>

Dirty Tactics (Special Weapons & Tactics 1)

Dirty Ballistics (Special Weapons & Tactics 2)

Dirty Operations (Special Weapons & Tactics 3)

Dirty Alliance (Special Weapons & Tactics 4)

Dirty Justice (Special Weapons & Tactics 5)

Dirty Trust (Special Weapons & Tactics 6)

Dirty Secrets (Special Weapons & Tactics 7)

Dirty Ultimatum (Special Weapons & Tactics 8)

<u>SWAT boxset, books 1-3</u>

<u>Trust & Honor Series (BWWM)</u>

Dallas

Dalton

<u>A Langdale Christmas</u>

The Christmas Secret

The Christmas Wish

The Christmas Gift

<u>Interracial Romances (BWWM)</u>

Pieces of Me

Hard Love

Retain Me

Silent Deception

<u>African American Romance</u>

Breaking The Rules

<u>Mafia Romance</u>

Unexpected Allies (The Tokhan Bratva 1)

9 781956 602999